FINNGLAS
AND THE STONES OF

"On, Cloud-Clearer, on!" screamed the princess Finnglas. But she knew her horse was already pouring out all his strength. And the black stallion was still ahead . . .

Finnglas is riding for her life. If she fails the first of the Seven Trials to win the kingdom she will die. And the Summer Land will never be free from the grip of the Druids and their Powers.

This is the third book about Finnglas and her friends, but it can be read on its own. The other titles are *Pangur Bán, the White Cat*, and *Finnglas of the Horses*. *Pangur Ban, the White Cat* was shortlisted for the Guardian Children's Fiction Award, 1984.

Fay Sampson is the author of thirteen books for children and teenagers. She lives with her family in a centuries-old Devon cottage, overlooking Dartmoor. As well as writing, she works as a part-time teacher of mathematics. She spends her holidays collecting material for her books – anything from Celtic archaeology on Iona to whale-watching.

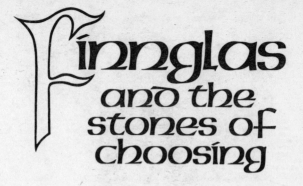

Finnglas and the stones of choosing

FAY SAMPSON

Illustrations by Kathy Wyatt

A LION PAPERBACK

Tring · Batavia · Sydney

Copyright © 1986 Fay Sampson

Published by
Lion Publishing plc
Icknield Way, Tring, Herts, England
ISBN 0 7459 1124 2
Albatross Books Pty Ltd
PO Box 320, Sutherland, NSW 2232, Australia
ISBN 0 85648 815 3

First edition 1986
All rights reserved

British Library Cataloguing in Publication Data
Sampson, Fay
  Finnglas and the stones of choosing.
  I. Title   II. Wyatt, Kathy
  8.23′.914[J]   PZ7
ISBN 0 7459 1124 2

Printed and bound in Great Britain
by Cox & Wyman Ltd, Reading

To Elizabeth

It was the dawn of the day on which Finnglas should be chosen queen.

But no one saw the sun rise. Grey mist hung low over the fortress of Rath Daran. You could not see its blackened ruins. The smell of smoke hung heavy in the air.

The princess Finnglas stood in the doorway of the house set apart for her. She was not dressed in the finery of a princess. There were no ornaments of gold in her long damp hair. She had wrapped a plain grey cloak around her against the rain. But she raised her face proudly towards the clouded hills.

She had been three years away from the Summer Land. Yesterday she had come home to a blazing palace and held her dying father in her arms. Somewhere up there, beyond the clouds, was a higher hill, the Place of Choosing. At noon today she must place her foot on the rock between those two tall stones and hear the tribe cry out her name:

'*Finnglas of the Horses! Finnglas of the Horses!*'

'Are you afraid?' said a deep voice behind her.

She turned with flashing eyes.

'Have a care! It is you who should be afraid, Niall Cross-Bearer. The Chief Druid, Dubhthac, has no love of Christian monks.'

The burly young man in his brown monk's robe flushed and grasped his wooden cross for courage.

'Your father trusted us to help you. We will not fail you.'

Finnglas looked round at her four friends. Niall, the monk. Erc, a red-haired boy her own age, who had been a fisherman's son. His mother Ranvaig, once the dead king's slave. And at her feet in the wet grass, a small white cat called Pangur Bán, lifting his face to listen to her.

The princess could not resist a smile.

'With friends like these, how could I be afraid?'

Ranvaig drew a knitted shawl over her grey hair.

'You speak truer than you know. Four loyal friends are worth more than a faithless army. Come, princess, before you can be queen, we must bury your father with honour.'

They came down through the mist to the sea-lough and the harbour. A huddle of fishermen's houses shadowed the water. Out of the gloom came the keening song of women wailing and bursts of men's voices in loud argument. Finnglas caught her own name, with others of the royal house.

'You are a quarrelsome people in the Summer Land,' Niall muttered. 'Can they not hold their peace until your father is buried?'

A tall, hooded figure stepped forward in front of Finnglas. For a moment, she did not recognize him. For this grim ceremony, Dubhthac, the Chief Druid, had shrouded his white robe beneath a black cloak. But where the folds parted she glimpsed the silver crescent on his breast and caught the glimmer of the Golden Knife he wore always in his girdle.

'Welcome, daughter of Kernac,' he said without warmth. 'There is sorrow this morning, but joy comes with the noonday sun. It is time to sing your father on his last voyage. Will you take the second boat, with me?'

Finnglas looked round. A ring of nobles had formed, pushing forward, jostling for position. She saw their bristling beards and moustaches, beaded with dew. She heard their voices raised as they cursed and pushed one another. Heard the jingle of weapons. Like her, they had put aside their finery for this one morning and come dark-cloaked and plainly armed. But their pride they would never leave behind.

Only the dead king lay in a boat at the water's edge, dressed in his finest gold armour. He was wrapped in his royal, seven-coloured cloak, still singed and charred. Beside him lay his great two-handed sword, his shield, his harp.

She steadied her voice.

'I will ride with you, Dubhthac Golden-Knife. And with my closest friends.'

The druid's eyes sparkled with sudden anger.

'Do you insult your father? A foreign monk, a common fisher-boy and a slave-woman?'

8

Shouts of indignation rang round the ring of nobles, startling the sleeping swans and sending them hissing in fright across the water. Pangur Bán leaped on to a lobster pot, thankful that for the moment they had forgotten about a small white cat.

But Finnglas's answer flew back.

'Ranvaig was born a free woman. And my father restored her liberty with his last breath. She stays with me of her own free will. Erc and Niall have rescued me from death and dishonour. Never had princess nobler friends than these. And to Pangur the cat I owe more than any other — save one alone, Arthmael the great Dolphin, who saves us all.'

'So? You would bring strange ways to the Summer Land. The Dolphin's ways. It is not well. The Summer Isle is bound by ancient customs. It shall go ill with the land if they are broken. You will be telling us next you want the common people to have a share in the choosing of the Ruler. Would you have us ask the cat as well?'

An ugly laughter burst out around the circle. Pangur trembled on his lobster pot as they all turned to glare at him. Niall rested his hand on Finnglas's shoulder and said steadily, 'Let us not shame your father by brawling at his burial. There's a coracle over there that no one's wanting. It is big enough for the four of us.'

'The Island of Kings is not the place for such as them,' growled a scar-faced warrior.

'Those who insult my friends, insult me,' returned the princess dangerously.

In the tense silence that followed, the women stopped their keening to watch, and the men's hands shifted too easily to their weapons. It was Pangur who settled it. He leaped to the gunwale of the coracle, a small white figure crouched above the grey lough. Niall, Erc and Ranvaig followed him. No one stopped them, though many murmured.

Finnglas was left alone facing the druid Dubhthac. Pale and tight-lipped, she walked ahead of him and took her place in the second boat, behind the dead king's curragh.

2

They buried Kernac in the early morning, on Relig Rí, the Island of the Kings.

The king's body rode in the first boat on its final voyage. Six druids were its crew, their faces hidden by their hoods. Slowly the convoy put out from the shore to the beat of muffled drums. Grey mist hung low on the inlet of the sea below Rath Daran, the seaweed black on the rocks, and the drops of dew cold on the gunwales of the boats.

The princess Finnglas sat facing the Chief Druid Dubhthac in the second boat. She scorned to cover her head from the rain. Her proud face was set. Tears glistened in her eyes, but whether from anger or from grief, none could say.

More druids, warriors and bards filled the following boats. All the nobles of Kernac's court. They made a heavy music on the lough, with the thud of drums like slowly beating blood, and the thump of fists on covered shields and the keen of pipes. The oars dipped into the dull water, rose weeping and dipped again.

Last of all in the procession came the coracle with the princess's four friends. Erc rowed in silence. The others sat peering ahead through the mist at the low mound of Relig Rí, like a land of shadows coming nearer.

Niall laid his big, scarred hand on Pangur's neck and said uneasily, 'Look at the Chief Druid there. I wouldn't trust him. He has the eyes of a man who must have power.'

'But he promised Finnglas's father he would serve her as his queen. All the nobles did,' Pangur protested. 'We heard them swear it by King Kernac's deathbed.'

'But Dubhthac is a clever man,' said Ranvaig from the stern. 'And words do not always mean what they seem to mean.'

Niall nodded. 'The druid Dubhthac will serve the gods he knows. He has not danced with Arthmael, as Finnglas has.'

10

At the name of the great Dolphin, all four of them turned their heads to look down the long sea-lough. Mist hid the distant ocean. There was no break in the low, heavy swell. No dancing back. No Arthmael.

'Look out!' said Pangur, turning back to the bows, just in time. 'We are almost there.'

The leading boat touched on the stones of Relig Rí. Druids carried the king's body up the wet shingle and over the grass. Finnglas and Dubhthac walked behind it, and all the nobles after them. Across the water, black-clad women still mourned on the shore.

'I'm going nearer,' said Niall.

His broad shoulders worked their way determinedly towards Finnglas. His hands were placed firmly on his wooden cross. But Pangur ran faster through the damp grass, past the boots and hems of robes where only a small cat could squeeze. He rubbed his white fur round her ankles to comfort her.

They laid Kernac's body reverently on a stone slab. Then those of the royal blood stepped forward, one by one. His brother Manach placed the king's broken sword on his breast. Tomméné, his horse-master, carried his shield. His eyes were bright with tears. Young Rohan of the Chariots brought the magnificent trappings of his ponies, jingling like the distant music of another world. The pipers shrilled in a lament, as Laidcenn the Chief Bard rested the king's favourite harp beside the bier.

It was Dubhthac's turn. He signalled to the druids behind him. They brought him in their arms the old grey wolfhound who had been his master's delight. The grizzled head hung limply. The dog's throat had been cut.

'What is this!' cried Finnglas in horror. 'Who has done this foul deed?'

Dubhthac turned to her with a smile that did not warm his eyes. 'It is our custom, lady. Had you forgotten?'

'It shall be the custom no longer when I am queen. You shall lay no slain creature on my deathbed.'

'You are not queen yet, lady.'

'My father has named me *Tanist*, the heir to the kingdom.'

'Yet it is the nobles who must choose.'

Their eyes clashed like swords.

As they looked on, Erc gripped his mother's arm. 'What does he mean?' he whispered. 'They all promised, didn't they? They all bowed their heads to the earth and lowered their swords before Finnglas and swore to uphold her right. Would they betray her?'

'Hush,' murmured Ranvaig. 'There are many more that have come for this Day of Choosing. They did not all swear.'

It was true. Overnight, each of these nobles seemed to have grown his own circle, as swift-footed messengers had sped through the island with the rune-sticks that spelt Kernac's death.

Scarred warriors muttered to Finnglas's uncle, Manach. Old, seasoned horsemen held whispering council with Tomméné. Around Rohan of the Bright Chariots was a wild circle of young horsemen, like scarcely-broken stallions themselves, difficult to hold in check, flaunting their long hair and bright eyes even without their usual flash of jewels. And behind Dubhthac and Laidcenn the Harper were all the druids and bards.

Finnglas looked round at them all defiantly. Drawing herself up tall and proud, she walked into the open tomb. She laid a last kiss on her father's cold face.

Niall was edging nearer to the tomb. As Dubhthac raised the silver crescent to the sky and drew his golden knife across the air seven times, laments wailed from all sides, from the bards and the druids, driving the crows from the treetops. Niall broke through the ring, his wooden cross held high. His voice rang out confidently,

'*I am the Resurrection and the Life!*'

With an angry shout the druids rushed at him. His great, half-shaved head swayed and tossed among the flood of their hoods like an oak in a storm.

'Let him be!' cried Finnglas. 'It would be my father's wish. You saw his soul sail out upon the tide with the Dolphin.'

'The Dolphin does not rule in the Summer Isle!' ground Dubhthac's voice.

'He shall today, once I am queen,' Finnglas called back.

'Niall!' cried Pangur.

As the chanting, cursing druids fell back, the white cat leaped towards the monk. Niall lay felled and dazed on the ground.

At a swift sign from Dubhthac the stone ground into place across the tomb. From the opposite shore a wild chant of grief keened from the ranks of black-clad women beating their breasts.

> 'Ochone, Ochone!
> Winter it is now our king is dead.
> We are become like children without a father.'

But Tomméné mac Ruain leaped on to the top of the island and called in a ringing voice to all the tribe.

'Our king is dead. We fight each other like a herd without a stallion. I summon all who are of the royal house of Kernac, all who are noble, all the wise, to meet us at the Stones of Choosing at noon this day. The Stones shall tell the name of our new Ruler.'

> 'Ochone, Ochone!
> We are a ship without a steering-oar,
> We are a herd without a stallion.'

sang the women across the water.

'Aye! But only until noon!' Rohan of the Bright Chariots cried out to them. 'Then you shall have a new stallion, I promise you!'

Finnglas strode grimly to Niall and pulled him to his feet. Erc and Ranvaig thrust through the nobles to stand beside them. Finnglas's answer rang out proudly.

''No stallion, this time, Rohan of the Chariots. Today the Summer Land shall have a White Mare to lead it.'

But all the young men around Rohan laughed at her wildly and strangely.

The raindrops were already drying on the old king's tomb.
Now the morning sky was brightening towards noon. Young
Erc sprang to his feet as Finnglas stepped out of the house into
the sunshine. Niall and Pangur stared at the girl they thought
they had known.

Her hair was braided with silver, and golden apples swung
from the ends of the tresses. Her long dress was purple, tasselled
and thickly bordered with gold. Across her shoulders, a new
cloak of many chequers glowed in soft, bright wool, the clasp
richly fashioned of thick silver set with coral, like a marvellous
beast with a horse's head and a serpent's tail. The golden collar
on her throat, the golden arm-rings, all flashed in the sunlight.

'You look beautiful!' gasped Erc, and checked himself in
sudden shyness.

They had all drawn back from her a little, seeing her
suddenly look so much like a queen. All except Ranvaig, who
smiled in the doorway behind her.

Finnglas flushed a little and said hurriedly, 'I'm no
different. I'm still the same Finnglas. It's just the clothes. I
was happier when I wore a tunic and a sword.'

But they knew that she was not the same as them now. They
would never have to do what she was about to undertake.

Erc burst out, 'We cannot let you do this alone! The nobles
mean you ill. You heard them all muttering and laughing
together this morning. They do not mean you to be queen.'

'I know they promised King Kernac, your father,' said
Pangur. 'But do you think they might go back on their oath?'

'Never!' cried Finnglas in anger. 'You would not say that if
you knew the Summer Land. We are a people of honour!'

'I do not trust Dubhthac,' Niall protested. 'Erc is right. You
are going into great danger, Finnglas.'

'I tell you, they will keep their oath. And all the others must

14

then agree with them. The Stones of Choosing will not ring with the name of the ruler, unless they cry with one voice. It would be ill for the kingdom to be left without a leader. And Dubhthac will cry me queen more than any of them. Who should fear the power of a sacred oath more than a druid?'

'As long as you live to take the kingdom,' said Ranvaig quietly.

A moment of fear passed across Finnglas's face. But it was gone at once.

'Arthmael sent me here to be queen. He danced through death for us. We must be his partners in that dance now.'

'I wish Arthmael was here,' said Pangur, looking over his shoulder to where the spray was blowing sideways from the waves.

At the name of the Dolphin there was a small silence. Then Finnglas laughed.

'The courage of Arthmael is in our hearts, though we do not see him. Listen, they are summoning me to the Choosing.'

The sun was already high in the April sky. The drums were beginning to call.

All morning the chieftains had been coming. There were dust clouds on the road over the low green hills, and chariots bowling along behind the galloping teams, with spearmen riding after them. The horses might have walked along the grey glens from the north and the east and the west, but before they came in sight of the king's rath, there was not a one that did not whip his team to finish with a flourish. Kernac's tribe were a proud people who gloried in horses.

Some had come in ships, scudding along the coasts from white-foamed strongholds, spinning with bellying sail at the harbour-mouth and shooting on the wind into anchorage. Kernac's tribe were a proud people who never rowed where they could sail.

But others were coming quietly, down from the hills, or out of the deep forest. The druids walked, cloaked and hooded, women and men, with staffs as tall as themselves. They boasted no pride of chariots or ships. Yet the people moved aside from the road when they met, and lowered their eyes, and did not look again until they had passed. Sometimes there were pupils following behind them, sharp-eared and quick to learn. The pride of the wise was in their years of knowledge.

The nobles of the Summer Land were gathering to choose their Ruler.

The house that had been set apart for Finnglas was a lonely white-washed building, with a door that opened on the turf above the beach. As she walked across the fields towards Rath Daran she saw that a great crowd was already waiting for her. You could feel the excitement even from a distance. Children were dancing about at the edge of the throng.

'There is no hurry,' said Finnglas. 'It is a while yet to noon.' But it was her own quick steps she was steadying, not theirs.

Every head was turned to watch them. The Dolphin's friends were a little procession coming bravely across the grass to the waiting people. Finnglas first, just one step ahead of the others. Niall, his sandalled stride firm and determined, trying to look less worried than he felt. And Pangur Bán beside him, a small white cat feeling ridiculously exposed, with everyone looking at him. Behind them, Erc, grimly clutching the fisherman's knife on his belt, and Ranvaig, carefully watching every face as they came nearer.

All mourning clothes had been cast aside like the early clouds and the nobles shone out like Finnglas in their most brilliant finery. White-robed stood Dubhthac amongst all his druids, with the silver crescent on his breast and the golden knife at his side winking openly in the sunlight.

'Welcome, Finnglas of the Horses, to this Day of Choosing!'

Then the pipes shrilled out, and the procession was on its way.

The children were running beside them, calling excitedly, 'Finnglas! Finnglas of the Horses!'

Finnglas stole a glance around her. They were walking together now, those of the royal kin. Tomméné caught her eye, and he flashed her a sudden smile, white teeth wide against his black moustache. Happy memories flooded back from childhood. Of Tomméné lifting her astride her first, loved, piebald pony. Surely, Tomméné mac Ruain, of all of them, would name her queen?

The drums had settled to a steady beat, quickening now,

and her feet were quickening with it, drawing her towards the Place of Choosing faster than she might have wished to go.

She looked to her left. A shiver ran through her. Her uncle Manach, the master swordsman, his face stern and unmoving as his eye caught hers. She had learned from him all her skill in weaponry. Once before, he might have been named king, but they had chosen Kernac, her father. What was Manach thinking as he looked at her?

The procession was heading away from Rath Daran now, crossing a meadow where the cattle still browsed on the low winter pasture. Ahead was a second hill, the Place of Choosing, and on its summit, two upright stones pointing to the ever-brightening sky. The pillars of a gateway that led into a kingdom. The Way was beginning to climb.

Rohan of the Bright Chariots overtook her. The horsemen who had come galloping out of the hills had swelled his strength. She had seen the young men clustering thick behind him. They were all magnificent now, gold and bronze jingling from strips of leather like the harness of horses on parade. Rohan tossed his long red hair impatiently. One hand played restlessly with the jewelled dagger on his hip. The other was adjusting the bright gold clasp that held his cloak, turning it so that it flashed as it caught the sun. Oh, yes. This time there was no doubt of it. Rohan wanted to be king.

The Way snaked like a maze around the hill. Breath came fast and legs were aching, but the drums beat in the blood like a dance, and the pace did not slacken.

Laidcenn? But surely she did not need to fear the Chief Bard? In childhood she had sat on the grass with her brother, singing hour after hour the songs he taught them. From Laidcenn she could remember only love. And yet . . . A harper is a man of deep magic. If once he touched the strings of his beloved harp, which he called Cet Muinter, his Chief Wife, he could enchant the tribe to shout anything he wanted.

As they rounded a sharp twist in the path she sensed suddenly two other figures close behind her. There had been the sweep of a white cloak, the shadow of a black hood.

In that same moment the breathless bards skirled a last flourish on their pipes. The drums rolled out once more and

17

the skins were stilled. All movement ceased. They had reached the top of the hill.

The standing stones towered above Finnglas, with a slab on the grass between them, like a threshold. It bore a hollow, as it might have been the imprint of a foot. She watched the shadow of the Stones grow shorter and shorter on the sunlit turf. Then a horn blared out. The last edge of shadow slid beneath the Stones.

Dubhthac's golden knife flashed before Finnglas's eyes.

For one moment, Finnglas thought the knife was aimed at her. But Dubhthac chanted to the gods of soil and sky.

'By the Threefold Mother,
 By the Raven of Battles,
 By the good Lord of the Cauldron of feasting warriors . . .'

In a single movement all the tribe threw themselves face downwards on the turf. From every throat broke a wordless moan of fear. From old habit, Finnglas even felt her own knee beginning to bend. Then she remembered. She followed the Dolphin now. Arthmael bore the scars of bitter wounds. Her own hands had added to them. He had given his life to turn her from the path of blood and fear. She must not fail him now.

She stood before the Stones, looking down at all those bowed backs and outstretched arms. She stole a glance behind, and her spirits rose. She was not alone. Brave-faced amongst the prostrate ranks, Niall, Erc and Ranvaig kept firmly to their feet and their faith. Even little Pangur had leaped defiantly on to a boulder where everyone could see him.

Dubhthac was the first to raise his head. When he saw Finnglas still standing erect, he began to clamber to his feet, an expression of fury on his face. The Arch-Druid strode towards her. His finger stabbed at the princess.

'Again! What is this, daughter of Kernac? Have you come back to us so proud, you would challenge your father's gods?'

Finnglas willed herself not to back away. She tore her gaze from those fierce, hawk-like eyes, and forced herself to look instead at the grass-stained knees of his white robe. For a moment, she felt a wild desire to laugh. But on every side, warriors, druids, bards, craftsmen were rising from their knees. At the sight of Arthmael's friends still standing, the air was torn with shouts of anger.

19

Finnglas cried out, 'My father made his peace with the Dolphin. I own no Lord but Arthmael.'

'Strange and brave!' sang a wondering voice on her left.

Finnglas turned swiftly. A wave of joy rushed over her as she saw the calm face watching her. The woman was tall, taller than many men, with a staff as high as her head, bound in spirals of silver. She wore the white dress of a druid. For this one day, Sorcha of the Clear Sight had come down from the Mountains of Seeing, from the Place of the Stars. Looking at her, Finnglas felt again the frosty ground under her feet. Night after night she had stood beside Sorcha, watching the slow dance of the planets through the months and learning the names of three hundred and fifty-six stars.

Next moment she started violently. A second figure had crept between Sorcha and Finnglas. It was so close that Finnglas felt, smelt, rather than saw it. It was crouched and doubled, with a staff not straight like Sorcha's, but crooked, knotted and gnarled as the hand that grasped it. It was hard to tell what moved beneath that hooded cloak. But where the folds parted, a bunch of herbs hung from a girdle, stiff, black and withered. Only twice in her life had Finnglas seen that shape, yet with a shudder she named it now in her heart.

'Unlucky!' croaked a voice within the hood.

The yelling crowd fell silent instantly. Even Dubhthac held still to listen.

'Unlucky words. I say that blood must pay for this. The earth is hungry.'

A growl of rage thrilled from the throats of the druids massed behind Dubhthac. This time Finnglas could not disguise a shiver.

But from the back of the crowd, for the second time that day, Niall's deep chant thundered unexpectedly.

'The teeming sea, the fruitful earth,
Are singing of our Saviour's birth.
The crescent moon, the sun's bright ray,
Are heralds of a greater Day.'

The angry circle around Finnglas broke apart in tumult.

Every warrior's weapon was in his hand. Manach of the Hosts cried out,

'Does a stranger dare to raise his voice in the high ceremony of the King-making? Seize that priest and cut his tongue out!'

The terrified commoners fled before the flash of swords and daggers that rushed upon Niall. Pangur mewed shrilly, his claws bared and his fur standing on end. Only Sorcha stood unmoved.

'What new wisdom is this that you bring us?' her clear voice called over the heads of the warriors as she stared curiously at the defiant monk.

Niall stood his ground, the wooden cross held before him like a shield. Still he sang on, though his voice was beginning to shake.

> 'The mighty oak in forest dim
> Tells out the great Creator's hymn . . .'

'Silence him!' roared Manach.

The warriors burst through the fleeing crowd. Their brandished blades caught the noonday sun. Dark shadows fell across Niall's face. Erc sprang beside him, white and desperate.

'No!' shrieked Finnglas helplessly. 'Do not touch him!'

This time, she knew they would kill the monk.

It was Laidcenn who saved him. Before the swords could strike, his hand swept across his harp. The first chords throbbed through the stones like summer thunder. His fingers darted among the strings again, like a gale singing in the treetops. He played a last sweet run of notes, like a blackbird's song.

The blades poised in mid-air. The weapons wavered and dropped. The warriors began to tug at their moustaches in shame. A deep silence fell. The wind whistled across the hilltop. The circle was made whole around the Stones.

Reluctantly Dubhthac stepped back into his place. Old Conn stood on the other side of the Threshold. He was thin-haired and frail, the eldest druid, though not as wise as Dubhthac. In one hand he raised the white sceptre of the Ruler, the other held a circle of twisted gold.

21

'Nobles of the Summer Land, it is time to choose. I name before you now the house of Kernac, who was our king, and is our king no more:

'Tomméné mac Ruain. Manach of the Hosts. Laidcenn, Chief Bard. Rohan of the Bright Chariots. Dubhthac Golden-Knife, who is also Arch-Druid. Sorcha of the Clear Sight. And . . .' his old voice faltered, '. . . Gormgall, whom we call "the Fair". And Finnglas Kernac's daughter, who was once called Finnglas Redhand, but has come back to us as Finnglas of the Horses.

'How say you? Which of these will you have to rule you?'

There was an expectant silence. It was Tomméné who raised the first shout.

'I gave my word to Kernac. I name Finnglas of the Horses as my queen.'

From Kernac's warriors rose a ragged cheer.

'Finnglas of the Horses!'

She saw Manach, Rohan and Dubhthac all mouth her name. But Dubhthac's knife traced a strange pattern in the air, that seemed to give his words another meaning. Many of the nobles, whose faces she did not remember, stood silent. The Stones of the Threshold did not ring with her name.

It was Manach's turn. With his hand upon his sword-hilt, as one who remembers on oath, he called gruffly, 'For my brother's honour only, I name Finnglas, Kernac's daughter.'

Again the shout rang round the circle, but there were other nobles behind her uncle that bellowed. 'Manach of the Hosts!'

Still the Stones would not ring. The blood mounted in Finnglas's cheeks.

The choice had come to Rohan. He called out mockingly.

'Finnglas . . . of the Horses!'

And now the circle clashed with the chant of three names. 'Finnglas!' 'Manach!' But all the young men behind Rohan yelled, 'Rohan of the Chariots!' and burst into laughter.

Once more Laidcenn swept his fingers across Cet Muinter and stilled the uproar. But he laid the magic harp aside before his voice chimed,

'Finnglas.'

All the bards chanted forth in harmony,

22

> 'For salmon on the flooding tide,
> For deer upon the mountainside,
> For barley springing in the field,
> For golden milk the cattle yield,
> The name is Finnglas!'

But a cry of hate beat from the ranks of Dubhthac's druids like a fever burning in the blood.

> 'No!
> Cast her out or cut her out!
> Drive her out or drown her out!
> Hunt her out or hang her out!'

Their fingers were all pointing towards Finnglas. And now she could not help herself trembling, for she had been taught to believe such curses.

Sorcha Clear-Sight's voice echoed Laidcenn's in vain. The Stones could not ring true in all that tumult.

Then from close beside Finnglas, the cracked voice began to sing, as if it had once held some long-forgotten power to charm. The whole tribe fell silent, listening fearfully.

> 'Blood must be shed upon this Stone,
> Or blood will flow through all our lands.
> The kings who knew our ways have gone;
> These Stones will fall if Finnglas stands.

'I say we should put her to the trial.'

No one spoke. But Tomméné gave a violent shudder, as one who sees the heron that tells his death. Old Conn looked slowly round the circle.

'Is this the will of all of you?' he quavered.

There was a brief, uncertain silence. Then from all around the ring the nobles shouted,

'It is!'

Even Tomméné cried it, looking pleadingly at Finnglas, as though for release. And Laidcenn cried it, and all the bards, and Sorcha of the Clear Sight. As Finnglas had known they must, because the tribe must speak at last with one voice.

Dubhthac's eyes gleamed with triumph.

'Well, Finnglas of the Horses? So the Stones would not speak for you. Perhaps you are not fitted to be our queen. You were a child among us, in Kernac's palace and in your foster-home. You learned our ways. You knew the Old Powers. But you have been away from us too long. You come back to us with strange friends, and with a strange faith, following the Dolphin of the Scars. We feel these Stones begin to shake. The nobles doubt you. We would put you to the test.'

'What test is this?' Her mouth felt stiff and dry.

'The Seven Trials. They are, as it were, a challenge to a warrior, to single combat. Each night, for seven nights, you will be set a trial, to see if you remember the Old Ways. If you pass them, we shall cry you queen, seven days from now.'

'And if I fail?'

There was only the wind blowing through the trees.

Then Laidcenn's voice called softly across the circle. 'You will die. The Old Powers would destroy you.'

'Finnglas! You do not have to take this test!' Tomméné's warning rang urgently. 'On peril of your life!'

'Do you not trust her?' Sorcha laughed at him. 'Would you have the bards mock her from our shores as a coward? Have we not taught her well enough, you and I?'

'Daughter of Kernac, you must answer,' Old Conn still held the sceptre and the crown.

Her voice came low and clear.

'In Arthmael's name, I will take the Trials to win the kingdom.'

5

Finnglas lifted the heavy, carved gaming-board and set it on the table.

'Sit there,' she ordered Erc. 'I will teach you how we play the Game of the Hunt.'

She set out the pieces, white for herself, red opposing her. When the lines stood facing each other, she lifted a white hind with a golden collar. Her eyes flashed a challenge across the chequer-board.

'This,' she said, 'is the quarry. You must slay it, before it crosses the board and takes your kingdom. Are you ready? Then let the game begin.'

And she moved her first white piece out into the open. Slowly, Erc chose a red huntsman. The two pieces began to advance towards each other.

For a while their heads, his red, hers brown, bent over the board.

Then Erc said, without looking up, 'What did they call that old crone who stood beside you?'

Finnglas spoke the name low, as Old Conn had done. 'She is called Gormgall the Fair.' And there was not a trace of mockery in her voice.

'And she is kin to you?'

'My father's aunt. But they say that she has fairy blood in her. She is wise in things that even Dubhthac does not know. She brews the herbs of life and death.'

There was the sound of running footsteps on the grass outside. The doorway darkened suddenly. Something flew through the air and struck the floor in front of Finnglas.

Pangur had been sleeping on the sunny doorstep. He let out a screech and sprang into the air. Niall came running from the rock where he had been whittling wood. Ranvaig dropped a batch of hot loaves.

A young man with curly hair stood in the doorway, grinning and breathing hard. He touched his head and swept a low bow to Finnglas.

'From the High Folk of the Summer Land to Finnglas Redhand. Greetings!' And he turned and sped away towards Rath Daran.

Finnglas had risen in fury. 'Do they insult me? Does Alprann Wingfoot, my father's swift messenger, not stay for my answer? Is this how the kin of Kernac honour their queen?'

Erc's voice came strained from the corner. 'You will not be queen for seven nights.'

For a moment, no one moved. The message lay on the floor, where Alprann had tossed it. It was a rod of alder, newly-cut. The raw wood had not yet discoloured in the air. Along its length a single line was scored. On either side it was hatched with shorter marks like the feathered shaft of an arrow.

Then Ranvaig stooped and handed it to Finnglas. The girl's hands still shook with impatience.

'It is the ogham script. I was no great scholar. Read it to me.'

Niall took the rod in his fingertips uneasily and scanned the lines.

'Meet us before sunset, at the stable-yard of the royal horses.'

'Horses!' At that word, Finnglas snatched the rod from him and tossed it into the air, laughing joyfully. 'Horses! Then it is Tomméné who sets the first trial. Praise be to Arthmael! This night I cannot fail!'

Ranvaig quickly made the sign to avert evil. Pangur growled low. Erc and Niall caught each other's eye in silence. Finnglas swung round on them all angrily.

'What are you staring at me for? Don't you understand? They call me Finnglas of the Horses. And they do well. In all the world that is what I understand the best. Even Tomméné, who taught me to ride, cannot surpass me here. This is one test I need not fear. Do you doubt me?'

'Only Arthmael knows what will happen.'

Quietly Ranvaig turned away and began to gather the fallen

loaves. But Erc lifted a red-robed figure from the board and moved it one step forward behind the huntsman.

Suddenly he burst out, 'Finnglas! Do not take this trial! I am afraid. You heard what the old crone Gormgall said. They want your blood.'

'Would you have me cried a coward? I am Kernac's daughter!'

'You are Arthmael's now. And Dubhthac hates the Dolphin. They will not let you win the crown.'

'Tonight they cannot stop me.'

Turning abruptly, Erc strode out of the door and stood staring, tight-lipped, at the sea.

Finnglas dressed carefully for that first trial. She put aside the long-skirted dresses from the clothes that had been laid ready for her, and chose instead chequered trousers, an embroidered tunic, and a short cloak of foxglove red that would not check her movements. Her feet were bare. When Ranvaig offered her a pair of short leather boots, she waved them away with a smile.

'No. It was thus I first rode a horse as a little girl. When I was too small to have any strength. I learned to ride, not by kicks and blows, but by being one with the horse beneath me. Feeling her, understanding what she felt. Letting my will flow into her through my hands and my thighs and my feet. I shall need all my horse-lore tonight. But I shall win.'

Proudly she came out in front of the others.

'So. I am ready. Will you come to watch me win my crown?'

Pangur crouched by the fire, staring up at her silently, as though he feared it might be for the last time.

Niall spoke for all of them.

'Don't you think you should be asking for a little help?'

An angry flush mounted in Finnglas's cheek. She left the house and, passing Erc without a word, she walked down to the shore.

'Arthmael!' she demanded.

The evening tide lapped gently on the stones.

'Arthmael? Don't be silly. I know you are listening.'

Without warning, one chill grey wave reared up in front of her and flung itself against Finnglas's legs. With a cry of

27

dismay she stepped back and looked down at her bright new clothes. The chequered wool of the trousers was dark and dripping, stained now with green weed, and mud, and wriggling shrimps.

'What did you do that for? Do you want to make me a laughing stock in front of my nobles?' she cried crossly.

The next wave broke further off. Finnglas watched it uncertainly.

'It's for you, I'm doing it. I don't want to be queen. You brought me back to take the kingdom in your name, didn't you? I must not fail you.'

A ripple of creamy bubbles caressed her bare feet. It drained away through the sand, tickling her toes. Finnglas's lips twitched in a smile. Then her face collapsed and she fell on her knees on the wet shingle.

'Arthmael, help me! I cannot tell the others, but I am afraid!'

The sea hissed gently all about her. The level sun shone dazzling in her eyes.

She walked up the hill to Rath Daran with her four friends. It seemed as if the whole tribe was waiting, with their faces lit by the sunset.

Kernac's stables had been burned to the ground in the fire that had killed him. Now his horses were picketed in a long line below the rampart walls. Finnglas walked past them towards the ranks of waiting nobles, murmuring half-forgotten names as she went.

Seven horses had been untethered. Young warriors held their heads. Finnglas's heart rose as her step quickened towards them. These were royal animals, gloriously bred.

'Greetings, Tomméné mac Ruain,' she called gaily. 'You offer me fine horses.'

In the warm rose of the sun's last rays, beads of sweat shone on the warrior's brow.

'You come at a good hour, Finnglas Redhand,' he said, as though they were lines he had learned. 'The people of the Summer Land have no king to ride out before them.'

'I am my father's daughter. I can ride where he has ridden,' Finnglas answered. And it was as though they were words she had known all her life.

The sweat began to trickle down Tomméné's face.

'Then you will take this trial?'

'Aye, and gladly.' Her eyes were sparkling. 'So! You would race me for my father's kingdom, would you? Which mount is mine?'

His words came halting, as though he would unsay them.

'No, princess. I may not choose your horse for you. Therein lies your trial. If you would race for the kingdom, you must know the horse that is fit for a queen. And . . .' He paused to swallow. 'I must warn you . . . There *is* only one.'

It was not what she expected. She did not hear Erc's gasp behind her for the sudden pounding in her ears.

She had thought only of the race ahead. Confidently she had dreamed of warm horse-flesh between her knees. Felt her hair stream back like the flying mane and tail of her steed. Believed that the horse and the wind and her own skill would all become one. Seen Tomméné laugh into his black beard as she swept past him to the finishing line.

But that was not the true test. And what it was appalled her. Her eyes raked the line of waiting horses. She felt their eyes, and all the eyes of her people, fixed on her. So simple a question, to choose one horse. Only her life hung on that choice.

She heard Niall mutter a prayer beside her. She glanced round at their strained faces and then turned back. If she chose wrongly, she would never see her friends again.

Tomméné was speaking to her. But she could not tell what he was saying. Her glance went past him to the sunset waters of the bay. The waves danced for her. She drew a deep breath. She must not panic. All the knowledge she needed lay already in her heart. They only wanted to see if she remembered.

She walked beside him to the beginning of the line, and the level rays of the sun caught the first horse. Finnglas drew a sharp breath. A pure white colt. He was perfect. A glorious strength and grace waited to flower in the arch of his neck and the sweeping lines of his head. An unblemished white horse was the sacred emblem of her tribe. Not long ago he would have been set apart for sacrifice; the horse of the gods.

It must be a trick. He was flawless. They had put him first, thinking that for that reason she must walk past him. But she was not so easily fooled.

'How old is he?' Her voice shook a little.

Tomméné glanced anxiously at the knot of druids at the far end of the line. One tall figure nodded. Dubhthac.

'Two years,' the warrior said hoarsely.

'Has he been backed?'

'No one has ridden him yet.'

He would be hers alone. She would be the first one ever to ride him. The only one. Her heart leaped within her. She would be a young queen on a pure white colt riding to victory in a Summer Land that would be made new under her rule. A clean beginning.

Suddenly, she laughed out loud and threw her arms round the colt's neck.

'No, little princeling! Beautiful you are, as May-time. But you are not for me. It would not be fitting. I shall be a new queen, untried, unschooled. Like you. A young queen needs an old horse to teach her wisdom. Take the colt away, but raise him royally.'

She threw a smile of mischief at Tomméné, feeling she had done well. But his face told nothing.

They moved on, and the low sun threw the long shadow of a mare in front of her. She was powerfully made, wide-shouldered and strong-chested. Her coat was dappled silver and her flowing mane and tail coal-black. She was just at her prime. Her nose reached down and butted Finnglas coaxingly.

Finnglas's hands ran along the mare's sides, feeling through the thick winter coat for the willing muscles. Her movements slowed. When her fingers came away they were not smooth with grease. She felt again. The hair, that should have been soft and silky, was harsh and dry.

Peering intently in the dying light she parted the coat. The neck was flecked with sweat. She rolled back an eyelid. Even in the golden sunset the eye looked yellowish.

Finnglas swung round angrily. 'What trick is this? Would you have me stake my kingdom on a sick horse?'

Tomméné cried hastily, 'It is nothing, princess! She will be well by morning.'

'We race tonight. Why have you brought her here to stand out of doors at nightfall when the dew is falling? Is this how the people of the Summer Land care for their horses?'

She threw the halter to the young horseman who had been holding the mare.

'Take her to your own stables and give her shelter. I will come to her myself in the morning, when my race is won.'

She swung back to Tomméné, challenging him to approve. But he was already walking on to the next horse.

As she followed him, a hand seemed to grasp her heart, twisting it. It was so startlingly like. A piebald pony, the mirror of her own first, loved, lost horse. The same floating islands of white on sleek black sides. The white-blazed nose. Bright, friendly eyes. She could not help herself.

'*Melisant?*' she whispered.

But Melisant was dead.

'This one?' asked Tomméné huskily.

They both knew that if he tried to guide her they would die together. The choice must be hers alone. She tried to steel her heart, and moved around the pony searchingly. Yet swiftly too, because the sun was sinking. She could find no fault.

The temptation was terrible. He was giving back to her all she had lost. The two ponies must have been bred from the same blood. The same markings, the same movement, the same height . . .

The cruel realization almost choked her. Three years had passed. Finnglas had come home a tall young woman. She turned her face away. She could hardly trust herself to speak.

'That was an unkind trick, Tomméné! Did you think my heart would blind my judgment? I am not a child now. The pony on which I first learned to ride will not serve me as a woman and a queen.'

This time it was she who turned her back on him and strode on along the line. Tears misted her eyes.

The sunset shone behind a copper stallion, making a golden halo of his mane. She blinked her tears away and eyed him warily. What trick had Tomméné played on her this time? He looked a noble animal. Generously made, a proudly-carried head, deep, liquid eyes. She made the young warrior who held his bridle walk him, trot him, gallop him, and uneasiness grew. She could see nothing wrong with him. No, that was too grudging a judgment. He would have been thought splendid beyond compare, in a land less famous for its horses.

He halted before her and leaned down his long nose. He blew warmly against her neck. Almost absent-mindedly she reached up a hand and fondled his silken mane. But all the time her eyes were sliding sideways, drawn irresistibly to the end of the line and the three magnificent horses still waiting for her. A lump of panic was rising in her throat. How could she choose between these four?

'Is this your choice?'

Tomméné's voice was tight with tension. She stared dumbly into his face, but it told her nothing.

'I don't know . . .' she muttered. 'Hold him here. I must see the others.'

All the gay confidence had drained from her. The copper stallion watched sadly as she walked away.

But Finnglas's heart leaped when she saw the second stallion. He reared night-black against the fading golden sky. She saw pride like her own in his high-groined, springing quarters, that small, fiercely-tossing head, the feathered feet that pawed the turf with sharp, shelled, polished hooves. He was all power and beauty and spirit, with gathered muscles that strained against the youth that held him back.

'Ride him!' she cried eagerly. 'Let me see him go!'

Enviously, she watched the groom vault on to the stallion's back and urge him forward.

He went like the wind, down the chariot-ground, round in a storming turn of spinning grass and peat, flying back to Finnglas in sparks and thunder. Her muscles clenched, feeling in imagination that power surge through her, longing to rule it and bring it under her command. Her eyes were shining as she stepped out to greet his rushing glory.

The crowd screamed. For a moment she thought that he would ride her down. The youth barely hauled him to a straining check just in front of her. Boldly she saluted this wild, free spirit.

'Glorious, glorious!' she cried, reaching up her arms to the stallion. He threw up his head, and the sharp black hooves reared before her face and plunged again. She grasped his bridle firmly.

Still holding him steadily, she swung round to Tomméné, longing in her face. But as she did so, her eyes swept past the ranks of druids, close to her now. They were observing her, waiting silently, all their dark gaze fixed to see what she would do. Her eyes met Tomméné's anguished look. Less certainly, she turned back to the black stallion.

His eye rolled dangerously and his teeth were bared. Flecks of foam spattered the corners of his mouth. The bridle fell from her hand. A black and bitter disappointment engulfed her. She closed her empty hands and forced her voice to stay low and steady as she spoke to the stallion.

'Are you still so angry? In the cool of the evening, after a hard gallop? Then you are not the horse for a queen. I could not trust you. Full of fire you are, as a stormcloud, and as dangerous. If I were just a princess, I would gallop proudly with you to the end of the world. But how would you bear me in the noise and heat of battle? How should I ride you when I am wounded and weary? A queen must think of more than herself and her horse. You would take my strength from me when I need it most. Lead him away.'

It was done. She had sent him away, though her thighs still ached to feel that power between them, and her hands still tightened as though they gripped his reins.

And now there were only two left, and her feet seemed to be drawn towards them like leaves sucked by the wind. In all her life she had never seen such a pair of horses.

They would have been matchless if they had not been matched to each other. They were flawlessly formed. Their coats were pale gold, with manes of falling silver. Like milk and honey, like the evening star hung on the harvest moon, like a bright sickle in a field of ripe corn. Their necks arched high, but their faces were loving. They were brave-spirited, yet schooled to courtesy.

Finnglas moved round the two horses in the evening light, her hands appraising them, while the crowd whispered like the wind through grass. Behind the pair stood the knot of druids, closely ranked, watching her. She glanced back at the copper stallion, but it was as if the choice lay between only two horses. So perfectly paired were the golden twins that they seemed like one. She could not separate them. And yet she must. Beautiful though they were, all these horses save one carried the gift of death. But which was it? The light was dying fast.

'Let go their bridles,' she commanded on a sudden impulse. The pair threw up their heads to the darkening sky. Finnglas called once to them. They broke into a canter, shoulder to shoulder, moving in harmony. She whistled another high command and the canter became a gallop, thundering, free. And yet, when she called again, they both turned in a single, flowing movement, matched stride for stride as they sped back. As they flew past her, their outstretched necks seemed to strain to reach the same fleeting point.

She cried once more, and the pair wheeled in one moment and came trotting back to her feet. They stopped in the same heart-beat, with hardly a handsbreadth between them, and reached out their noses to receive her praise. She gave it gladly. They were marvellous horses, the finest-schooled she had seen in her life. Magnificent, yet sweetly-mannered. True princesses. But her heart was beating like a frightened bird. There were two of them, as like as twins. And she could choose only one.

There must be something between these two. They could not be so absolutely equal. One of them must be a heartbeat older, a hairsbreadth taller, the coat more perfect by a single tuft. Yet, as she looked desperately from left to right, she knew that she would never see another pair in which each was so flawlessly the mirror of the other.

She tried to see them as a chariot-team, to picture them wheeling as they took the turn.

'When you harness them together, which one . . . ?' she started to say.

And then she knew. Even before she saw the anguish in Tomméné's face. She threw back her head with a clear, ringing laugh and tossed the bridles to the two young warriors.

'I cannot part them. No, I *must* not part them! I never saw a pair so perfectly matched, that moved with one step, thought

35

with one mind, loved each other with an undivided heart. What would the horsemen of the Summer Land say of me if I split the finest chariot-team in the western world? Could the queen take one and leave the other alone?'

She strode back to the copper stallion. She must choose now, while the light still held and her judgment was sure. Gravely she saluted him.

'This is the horse I choose. He is a great prince. My warriors will be proud to ride beside me, but he is not so glorious that they need be breaking their hearts for envy of me. A horse like this will give me strength, not rob me of it. In the heat of the day he will bear me bravely; when I am weary he will carry me tenderly; if I fall he will cover me. A queen could trust her life to such a horse.'

'And so you shall!' The great stallion threw up his glossy head and neighed a welcome.

'Shame on me, but I have forgotten his name.'

'He is Sailte Cloud-Clearer.' Tomméné's eyes were bright with tears. She did not know what they meant. 'Is he indeed your choice, princess?'

'He is.' But what did that ripple through the ranks of druids warn?

'Then you and he must race me for the kingdom . . . Bring out for me the black stallion!'

A sudden doubt engulfed her. The black stallion? In the darkness of fear she knew it was too late to change her mind. She threw a swift glance at the chestnut stallion behind her. He was a noble horse. But could he outrace the keen, swift, dangerous black?

Sailte butted his shoulder against her, warm and reassuring. She put her arm around him, aware that he must feel her trembling.

'Mount,' he whispered into her hair. 'Do not be afraid. I will gallop for us both till my heart bursts.'

She was the rider. It was her place to give courage to her horse. Yet, as she settled herself astride his broad back, she felt his strength flowing into her muscles, the warmth of his heart comforting her bare, cold feet, the power of his will gathering itself under her hands.

Tomméné flashed a wild strange look at her from the back of the plunging black. He was very pale. Finnglas's throat tightened. She had so longed to ride that stallion. How would she have felt now if she held him beneath her instead of Cloud-Clearer? Her life hung on this choice.

The sound of the crowd had been roaring in her ears like the wind. Now silence fell. It had all taken place so quickly. As if her own short life were galloping to its close. No time for farewells to the friends she loved. She threw them a quick, brave smile.

'Are you ready, my lady? Tomméné mac Ruain?' Old Conn the Druid held up his arm.

Sailte drew a quivering breath and lifted his head. The black's hooves danced with impatience.

Conn's white sleeve flashed through the air. Before the princess's heels could strike his sides Sailte leaped away. Finnglas threw herself low on his neck, lightly poised. She gave herself willingly to his flying power. He needed no urging on. She heard only the wind rushing past her ears. She was deaf to the yells of the crowd, blind to everything but the golden flames of Sailte's mane blown back in her face and the grey-green turf hurtling endlessly towards her.

They were spinning on the first turn when a shadow passed her eyes. She could not hear the second hoof-beats above the pounding in her ears. But the black nightmare of Tomméné's stallion swooped past against the yellow glare of sunset.

'On, Cloud-Clearer, on!' she shrieked, drumming with her heels. But she knew he was pouring out his utmost store of speed. Still his neck lengthened in one tremendous effort. She did not need to look sideways now. Tomméné's black horse was galloping in front of her. Sailte's huge gasps felt as if they were torn from her own lungs. He swept wide on the second turn to avoid the black, and she heard the crowd groan.

Desperately he clung to the black stallion's heels, though divots of turf showered into his face. Through the flying mane Finnglas saw the starting-line rushing towards her again. There was a mass of faces, people pressing dangerously out into the track. Instinctively her hands tightened on the reins to steer Sailte aside. But ahead of her, Tomméné and the dangerous black tore unswerving as a lightning bolt along the straight. The crowd leaped back. Finnglas gulped with relief as Sailte's flowing stride went leaping past unchecked. She caught a glimpse of bright red hair and the white face of Erc.

They reached the top of the straight for the second time. Still Sailte's effort had not slackened, but stride by stride Tomméné's mount was pulling away further and further still. Finnglas gave herself utterly to her horse, making herself as low and light as possible. She could only trust Sailte now, though it seemed unthinkable that he could close that gap. Somewhere on the edge of her mind she wondered what would happen to her when the race was over. There was not time to imagine that.

Sailte hurled himself round the last turn as though his legs had found a new lease of strength. There were three lengths between the horses now.

'Faster, Sailte!' she urged vainly. She could not help herself.

He did not deserve that. She could see the veins swelling, stretching, straining, hear his thundering heart. He was the bravest horse she had ever ridden. It was not his fault. But his courage alone was not enough to match the speed of the black.

She laid her head along his neck and murmured 'Thank you.' She did not know if she would be given time for that at the end.

When she lifted her eyes again she saw with a shock the tall figure of Dubhthac at the edge of the track, his arm uplifted. They were nearing the finishing line already. The black stallion was leaping ever further in front. It seemed that his flying hooves must leave the ground and carry him up into the gathering stormclouds.

The crowd was screaming wildly. The common people seemed to be crying her name. But Dubhthac the Druid stepped out across the paths of the horses as if to hail Tomméné as the winner. His robe shone white before the darkening sky. And the level sun blazed triumphantly in the crescent moon on his breast. As the mirrored light flashed out in the eyes of the oncoming horses, the black stallion screamed in terror. He reared wildly, plunged and leaped again. Sailte Cloud-Clearer was almost upon him. Startled, Finnglas tried to recover her seat and haul him back. But in a smooth, sure-footed surge of speed Sailte wheeled to his right and passed him. Tomméné, like a plunging crow, went cartwheeling across the sunset sky. Then he and the fallen black stallion were gone from Finnglas's sight, and Sailte's neck was stretched out eagerly, his last strides swallowing the ground, and all the tribe were cheering them past the waiting line of druids.

They seemed to go galloping on together still, as though their wild ride would never end. But at last Sailte slowed, stumbled and recovered himself. She felt him trembling as she wheeled him round. She could not speak, only she found herself patting his neck, over and over again. The sound of the crowd was like distant breakers as they trotted back. Then they were all around her and roaring her name.

Niall lifted her down and hugged her fiercely. Erc, his face glowing with happiness, grasped her hand. Ranvaig was stroking Sailte's nose. The crowd was yelling 'Finnglas! Finnglas of the Horses!' over and over again.

The princess turned and took the red cloak from her shoulders. With her own hands she wiped the sweat from Cloud-Clearer's face and dried his neck. Gravely she saluted him.

'Honour to you, Sailte Cloud-Clearer. I did better than I knew when I chose you. In our first hour together you have saved my life.'

He could not speak. The breath was still gasping in his throat. But his liquid eyes were bright with love. Then the crowd parted behind Finnglas, and Tomméné limped towards her. He went down on one knee, unsmiling.

'You chose well, princess. Tomméné mac Ruain names you his queen. And it is well you did. If you had chosen falsely . . .'

Dubhthac was beside him, cold and grim.

'Tell her, Tomméné mac Ruain. Let her see what would have happened if she had chosen any other horse.'

The ranks of druids moved their white robes aside. On the grass behind them waited a strange, sharp plough. Its blade glinted in the cold, yellow sunset, oddly curved and silvered.

Tomméné gulped. 'If you had chosen falsely, that horse you named would have been yoked to the Old Ones' plough. We . . . I should have driven a furrow over you. The land you claimed would have drunk your living blood.'

In the silence that followed, Pangur's cry was the only sound.

8

Niall sat by the fire, carving a piece of hollow driftwood.

'There are footsteps,' he said. Even as he lifted his head, the second summons fell in the doorway.

'Be at the Oak of the Keepers in the Great Forest, when the dusk falls.'

Ranvaig looked up sharply as he read it out. 'This is no warrior's test. It is one of the Wise this time who calls her to the Oak of the Old Ones.'

'Where has Finnglas gone?' asked Erc suddenly.

'She went to tend the dappled mare who was sick last night.'

'That was long ago,' Niall said. 'She should be back by now. I'm going to look for her.'

The young monk found the princess in the stable-yard. She seemed to be grooming Cloud-Clearer. But her face was buried in his mane and her shoulders were shaking.

He put an arm round her. 'What's wrong? You passed the first trial nobly. You have won a fine friend. They do well to call you Finnglas of the Horses.'

Her voice came muffled.

'And that is why I am afraid.'

'You? Afraid?' he laughed. 'I never thought to hear Finnglas say that!' There was no answering smile in the face that she swung round to him.

'Can't you see? Yes, they call me Finnglas of the Horses. And they do well. In all the world, horses are what I know best. All my life I have lived with them, worked with them, loved them. Here at Rath Daran and in my foster-home. That should have been the easiest of the seven trials. And yet I almost failed. When I saw the black stallion and those golden twins . . . Forgive me, Sailte! I nearly passed you by.'

The chestnut horse snorted caressingly against her neck.

'But you chose truly in the end. You did not fail.'

'Tomméné is my friend. He set that test. And it was hard for me. What trial will my uncle Manach set? Or Rohan?' Her voice fell to a whisper. 'Or Gormgall the Fair?'

Niall did not answer for a while. He sat down on a pile of straw, and his hands were busy finishing the thing he was making.

Finnglas looked round slowly.

'It's not for myself! Never think that. I'm not afraid to die for Arthmael. But oh, Niall, what if I fail him? What if he has brought me here to be his queen, and I am not wise enough or good enough? What if Dubhthac wins, and it is all my fault, and the kingdom is handed back to the powers of darkness?'

Niall said nothing, but went on carving. Presently a low note twanged through the air. And then another, higher. A scale rippled briefly, changed pitch, and broke into a throbbing psalm.

'What is that you have there?' she asked, hiding a hiccup.

Niall looked down at the wooden lyre nestling against his shoulder. He stroked the strings proudly, and a carol sprang from them.

'It's nothing much. Just a six-stringed crot. Nothing so fine as the instruments your harpers play.'

'But where did you find it?'

The big monk flushed. 'Oh, here and there. A piece of driftwood on the beach, hollow as a soundbox, with branching arms that met to hold the strings. And Sailte Cloud-Clearer gave me hairs from his noble tail to plait for them. The pegs I carved from sheep's-bone.'

'You *made* it?'

'Once I was a painter of Gospels. There are no manuscripts here. And my hands would always be making something.'

'Play it for me.'

He plucked its strings, and his deep voice began to chant a hymn.

Finnglas turned back to her grooming, with rhythmic sweeps of the gold-backed, bronze-toothed comb. Sailte stood patiently under her hands, whickering softly into her shoulder to the thrum of the strings.

As the last note died away, Niall held out the lyre to Finnglas. 'It's your turn now.'

She took it unwillingly. 'I was never as fine as a princess or a harper should be. Now my nails are broken with three years building and sailing. I cannot pluck the strings with them. And I have forgotten all that Laidcenn ever taught me.'

All the same, she tuned the pegs and tried the six notes.

'What shall I sing?'

'Anything you know. It will come back to you.'

'This?

> 'Seven chiefs rode out of the wood,
> When the black bull was running.
> The sun shall set in a river of blood
> Before they chain his horns . . .'

She laughed. 'I'm sorry. That's all I can remember.'

'They taught you bloodthirsty songs in the Summer Land,' remarked Niall drily, as he began another hymn. Erc, Ranvaig and Pangur Bán had come silently into the yard to listen. Niall passed the lyre to Erc.

'Now you.'

'I cannot play. I'm a fisherman, not a royal bard. I didn't go to school like you two.'

'Don't fishermen sing songs?'

He snatched it from the monk. Roughly, whistling to cover his mistakes, he tried to pick out a shanty, such as sailors might chant as they hauled their nets in. Then his voice broke.

'You don't know what you're asking! How can I play a jig when Finnglas may be dying tonight?'

He threw the crot down in the straw and ran through the gate. Finnglas stood staring after him as he fled along the beach. Then Ranvaig picked up the lyre and shook the chaff from the soundbox. Slowly, as if her fingers were stiff, she plucked the strings and began to sing a plaintive lullaby.

When she had finished, Pangur swallowed. Finnglas blew her nose.

Then she felt Niall touch her arm. He was offering her the lyre again.

'Take this,' he said. 'Music is healing. Why don't you go down to the shore and sing for Arthmael? He will understand.'

They watched her walk away from them out over the rocks, slowly, as though a great weight lay on her shoulders. They saw

43

her sit, with her chin close to her knees, hunched in the wind. Heard the first wandering notes and saw the dolphin's blowhole rise quite close to her, and then a wide, wet grin.

'Come,' said Niall, picking up Pangur. 'Let's leave them alone.'

Finnglas finished her lament. Arthmael leaped out of the water and clapped his flippers together.

'Bravo!'

He fell back into the swell and rose again. He laid his beaked head on the wet stone beside Finnglas.

'Well, go on. Sing something else. I enjoyed that.'

'I don't know the right songs. I wasn't taught hymns and psalms like Niall.'

'Listen.'

His blowhole opened, and out came a series of squeaks and whistles, warbling off key. A small bright eye winked at her.

'There! Did you enjoy that?'

Finnglas managed half a grin. 'Not much.'

'But that is all a dolphin knows. Sing me what *you* know. I'm not fussy.'

'Where shall I start?'

'What's wrong with the beginning?'

So she began with the three daughters of the Great Mother, coming through the waves to the Summer Land. Of silver branches bearing golden apples, drawn in a chariot of foam by singing swans. Of the first white blossom planted and flowering in a new green land, like fallen stars.

She sang of kings and queens, and of her father's deeds, and all the tales that came pouring back from childhood. And as her fingers grew sure, and the magic, remembered, flowed from the harp, the dolphin rose up on his tail and danced for her.

All afternoon the waiting friends listened to the snatches of song on the wind. The high, brave voice singing from the seashore, and Arthmael's laughter.

When she came in, she was still humming. She paused beside the gaming board. With a little smile, she moved the white hart forward and lifted a red huntsman from the board.

'The first one to us!'

But Erc did not come back till the songs were over and the dusk was gathering.

44

9

The tribe accompanied Finnglas to the Great Forest as the dusk fell. There was no singing now. Indeed, it seemed to the frightened Pangur that the crowd was smaller than it had been before. The common people huddled together with torches for cheer as they set out along the Deep Way. As they began to move across the shoulder of the hill, a noise broke out deafeningly, of horns and bells and clappers, to scare away what spirits might be lurking in the gloom.

And yet it seemed to Pangur that the flames were pale and the noise was small and the twilight beyond immense and threatening.

Presently they stood on the ridge above the Forest. The stars were pricking through the grey sky, but the Way dropped down, carved by thousands of feet, deep into the soft, black earth. The shadows of the Forest swelled up to enfold them.

'I thought it was dark above, but this is worse,' whispered Erc to Niall. 'We have lost the stars. I wish I was on the deck of an open boat. This is no place for a sailor like me.'

'Look out! You're walking into a holly bush,' hissed Pangur.

'It's all right for cats,' Niall grumbled. 'You're used to hunting in the dark.'

The torches behind them threw wandering shadows over the trees. Strange arms jumped out to claw them. Shreds of rag hung here and there from branches. Their footsteps fell deathly quiet on rotten leaves. Even the bray of horns and bells was uncertain now, as if those who carried them had suddenly become afraid of what they might waken.

'Listen,' murmured Finnglas, pausing for a moment on the downward path.

The procession halted. From deep below, in the heart of the

Forest, came the thud of drums. Slow, rhythmic, like a sleeping pulse. And yet, as they moved on again, it was hard not to let that pulse beat in their feet, drawing them deeper and deeper down into the shadows. Pangur brushed close against Niall's sandals.

The drums called faster now. Nearer and nearer. All noise behind them had ceased, save for the hurried breathing of frightened men and women.

'Eeee!' shrilled Pangur.

All the torches behind them went out suddenly, stamped in the damp soil. The accompanying tribe wailed and groaned in fear. There was a thin, grey light ahead, a clearing in the Forest. And at its centre, a massive Oak blotted out the stars. Even the sacred trees that circled it kept their distance, as they leaned their shadowing branches towards the centre. Yet it seemed to the watchers that they were more than trees. Their trunks had grown cavernous eyes, hollow cheeks, long cruel mouths.

The last of the light brushed the pale robes of smaller, human figures beneath them, the waiting druids and bards. Out of the darkest shadows under the Oak, sang a warm, gentle voice.

'Welcome, Finnglas. Have you come to gladden this evening with music for us?'

'Laidcenn the Harper!' gasped Pangur. 'I was sure it must be Dubhthac himself in a place like this.'

Finnglas stood still for a moment, as though she too was taken by surprise. She looked upwards. Over her head twinkled a crown of stars, caught between the encircling Forest and the unseen Oak at its pivot. She found her voice bravely.

'This is a solemn place for the bards to summon me. I would rather have heard you harp in my father's halls. But I have come here to do what the Wise Ones demand of me, and win the right to my father's kingdom.'

'Your father's hall is burnt. And much more was lost with him. Finnglas his daughter comes back to us singing strange songs. We do not know your Dolphin, but we feel the Oak begin to wither at its roots. The bards would heal it.'

'If the land is hurt, the queen shall bind its wounds. What is your challenge?'

'Make magic for us. Sing the Great Healing of the Tree.'

'What's that? Does she know it?' croaked Erc. 'How can she play anything in the dark?'

'Be quiet!' Niall gripped the boy's arm. 'Lend her all your strength.'

Laidcenn came towards her in the faint starlight. He offered her a harp.

'Play this as though your life depended on it. As indeed, it does.'

Her voice came just a little higher.

'This is a fine instrument. White maple, by the smoothness of it. With strings of bronze. But I cannot see to play it.'

'Then you must play it from your heart, as I have taught you. Let your blind fingers make us see the vision within you.'

She took it slowly, and settled it in the crook of her arm. A whisper ran through the grove and was caught up in the trembling leaves of the oaks.

Her very first notes were false. Even Ranvaig could not hold back a gasp of dismay. Pangur shut his eyes and shuddered for Finnglas's life. But she was only tuning the strings. There was a waiting silence.

'I am ready now,' said Finnglas quietly.

And she began to play to them.

Three notes rose slow and true. But the pause that followed seemed to last too long. Niall's hand clenched tightly on Erc's arm. Then as her fingers found the strings more surely, her clear voice began to sing out through the grove. Erc felt Niall's huge frame sag with relief. She knew this song. It was one of the melodies she had played to Arthmael. But never till now had he heard the words.

> 'There is a garden, flowering in gladness,
> Watered by a spring from the heart of the world,'

A low murmur of approval hummed from the bards.

She paused again. Her friends turned cold. Had she forgotten? Had she fumbled and lost her way in the dusk? The song climbed again, more boldly.

'Fed by the source of all living rivers,
    Rooted in the rock that will never give way,'

And now her fingers were growing nimble, beginning to dance over the harp.

'Soars to the sky the Axis of Heaven,
    Spreads wide its branches a Tree for our haven . . .'

'Be careful!' moaned Niall. 'Don't play so fast!'
But the notes were slowing already. The harp grieved as her voice sank low.

'. . . Bare its branches,
    Bitter its bark,
    Life for us,
    But death to him.'

There was a shout of protest from the bards, a howl of rage. Next instant they came rushing across the clearing towards her.
'That is not the song!'
'She sings of death.'
'Silence her!'
Ranvaig cried out, 'The poor child!' as they surged around her.
Erc cast himself head-first into the furious throng and was thrown aside.
But Finnglas stood playing as though she did not see them. Before the bards could reach her, she threw up her head to the stars and swept such magic from the strings that it held the onrush of their feet and stayed their outstretched arms, even as they lunged to tear the harp from her grasp. The music soared triumphantly over them and the whole Forest held its breath to hear her.

'. . . Now the blossom bursts from the wood,
    Now its leaves are crowns of glory,
    Under the pool the Salmon are laughing.
    The fruit is ripening for the Feast of Fools.'

Her voice sang on and the strings rang pure. And all the people of the Summer Land stood enchanted under the spell of her harping. The last notes fell on the listening air.

> '. . . When the summer comes
> That knows no ending,
> Stag and hounds, the Hunt and the Hunted,
> Shall dance together round the Tree of Life.'

Finnglas drew her hands over the strings and left them pulsing. Niall brushed the tears of joy from his eyes. A deep stillness held the grove. When the last echoes had died away, Laidcenn spoke at last. His voice came smiling through the twilight.

'Strange. That was an old song, but your words have made it new. Yet it was beautiful, Daughter of Kernac, and truly played. You have won your harp royally.'

His voice was no less sweet as he added, 'But if you had plucked one false note . . . I should have broken that string, and with it, choked all song from your throat for ever.'

'He was *smiling*,' shuddered Pangur. 'You could tell by his voice, he was smiling when he said it.'

They were sitting on the beach in the cold spring wind. Finnglas got up and walked out over the stones towards the sea. The others watched her. Out in the heaving waters of the bay they saw a dorsal fin lift between the waves and vanish. Finnglas sat down on a rock and waited. The dolphin rose, nearer, and slipped under again teasingly. Presently they saw the princess kneel at the edge of the sea, as though she was talking to someone earnestly.

'Let's leave them together,' said Niall, turning his back on them. 'Look, Erc is coming back from fishing.'

Erc beached his coracle in front of them. He tipped out a basket of shining, slithering fish at Ranvaig's feet. She slipped the bright gutting knife from her belt and set to work.

'What is Finnglas doing alone?' asked Erc. 'Is she all right?'

'She is not alone. But she is afraid she may fail the next trial.'

Ranvaig's knife paused. A drop of blood fell on the stones.

'Is it true? *Can* she fail?' asked Erc, turning very pale. 'If Arthmael wants her to be queen?'

'I do not know.' Niall tossed a stone between his hands, his eyes lowered. 'Once, I thought Arthmael could not die. But I was wrong. Yes, I think it is possible that Finnglas could fail. But you must never tell her that I said so.'

'Hush,' said Ranvaig.

Finnglas was walking back across the beach to them. Her face was serious, but her step was firmer now.

'Well, mistress,' Ranvaig called to her. 'Is a queen too proud to gut mackerel for dinner?'

'Give me a knife,' smiled Finnglas, 'and I will show you.'

Ranvaig threw it to her. The blade went spinning through

the air, wheeling against the grey sky. Finnglas fielded it cleanly. She tossed it up in the air and caught it again.

'This is a good weapon. It falls true to my hand, and it sits firmly in the palm.'

'It was a good smith that forged it, in the land of Senargad where I came from. They did not search me when they took me for a slave. I could have killed my way to freedom.'

'I would have done.'

'It was blessed for a tool, not a weapon. It knows its work well. The power of a good knife lies in the balance. Haft to blade. Then each cut falls cleanly, and the effort is light. With a knife like that, you could gut fish all day and still aim true. And I should know. I slaved long hours in your father's kitchens, before Pangur set us free.'

Finnglas slashed off the head of a fish with a single blow, and tossed it to Pangur. Then she slit the body and scraped out the guts. Erc got out his own knife and began to help her.

Finnglas grinned. 'Right, Erc, son of Erc! I will match you, mackerel for mackerel.'

Ranvaig watched their flashing blades and murmured, 'God grant that the blood of those fish be the only life you spill.'

They washed the mackerel and carried them back to the house. Finnglas stopped short. The gaming board stood facing them as they entered. The squares were crowded, the red pieces threatening the white. Finnglas took a red-robed figure away and stood looking down at it in her hand.

'A second huntsman gone.'

But she was not smiling now.

At noon, the third message came.

'Meet us in the dark of night, by the armoury.'

11

It was Manach's turn.

The smell of burning still lingered over Kernac's dun. Finnglas and her friends walked past the blackened heaps of her father's palace, the feasting hall, the storehouses, the stables. Darkness covered the swinging sea. Even the stars were hidden. The beaten earth was cold beneath Pangur's paws.

Finnglas had dressed carefully again, in the same tunic, but she had left behind the cloak that might have hampered her sword-arm, and she wore soft leather boots.

As they rounded the corner into the open yard, the crowd that had followed them broke into murmuring. The darkness was ruddied by sudden firelight. In the far corner, under the ramparts, the smith's forge was still standing. Light glowed in its doorway from the embers of the day's furnace. Beside it stood the king's treasure-house of weapons and armour.

The nobles were waiting for them in front of the smithy, black figures in the red light.

Homesickness twisted in Finnglas's heart. A longing for the golden days of childhood. How often had she spent the bright hours of sunshine on that field outside? Almost as soon as she could crawl she had come there to watch the warriors with their slashing swords. To see the javelins arch and thrust against the clear blue sky. To hear the thunder of the chariot ponies' hooves. And after noon, when the men's practice was done and the cuts salved and patched, they became like little boys playing a game of hurly, whooping and yelling as they chased the ball with flying sticks, bare-footed, light of limb, enjoying their speed and skill.

She had not thought to come back like this, to death and ruin, and these faceless men who watched her come in silence.

One of them stepped forward.

'Greetings, lady. So you have come to take up my challenge.'

It was her uncle. Manach, who had taught her to wield a sword, standing over the smith till he had fashioned one just the right length for her little arm. But it was never a toy, for the edge had been honed so that even then she could sheer through a hazel wand with a single blow. Manach, who had given her no quarter in practice, ever. Manach, who had once charged her to avenge her brother's death.

'But she can't fight him now!' Erc's voice rose high with panic. 'It's pitch dark. She can't see what she's doing!'

'Hush, boy.' Niall gripped Erc's arm more fiercely than he realized. 'She is of royal blood. She's as used to sword-fighting as you and I are to picking our teeth.'

But Finnglas's next words chilled even him.

'I have fought you, uncle, as many times as there are stars in the sky, both before I went to my foster-home and after. And I have never beaten you once. You gave me Cruimthann the Avenger. But the first time I struck in anger fighting the mermaids, I lost both the battle and my sword. Yet, if that is the test, I will take it.'

Erc trembled under Niall's grasp. But his mother drew out a bundle of knitting from her pocket and calmly twisted the wool around her fingers.

'You mistake me, Finnglas Redhand. If swordsmanship could have won me the kingdom, it would have been I who reigned and not your father. Yet, if you would rule these warriors, you must prove your right in single combat tonight.'

Finnglas hesitated. Did she suspect some treachery?

'You speak in riddles, uncle. And I see no weapons.'

'Show her, Luis Sunfire.'

The smith came from the forge, like a dwarf from a cavern. One shoulder was higher than the other. A bush of black, grizzled hair sprouted from a face scorched by fire. He wore a leather apron. He was a man of deep knowledge and magic.

Luis's arms were full of clinking weapons, clasped to his breast like dear children. He let them fall to the ground at Finnglas's feet.

'I made them all,' he growled. 'Their blades are yours to use.'

Finnglas stared down at them. They were barely distinguishable in the dying fireglow. A litter of long shapes, the faint gleam of metal on the shadowy ground. She was being asked to choose again.

'You would make it easy for me,' she said evenly. 'I see I shall not be led astray by the dazzle of jewels or the glint of gold. Indeed, I can hardly see at all.'

'Does it matter which one she takes?' mewed Pangur.

'Her life hangs on it,' murmured Ranvaig. She began to knit.

'It's not fair!' he hissed. 'How can she tell?'

'Perhaps the answer is not found by the eyes.' The needles clicked sharply in the quiet air.

Finnglas half turned. She could not have heard the words, but she stood listening for a moment to Ranvaig's needles.

Then she bent and felt at her feet for the sword hilts. One by one she lifted the long weapons.

She did not say a word. She was a black shadow on the open yard. The four friends did not know what she was thinking. They only saw her stoop, and test a blade, and stoop again. Not being swordsmen, how could they guess what she was doing? Only Ranvaig knitted as she waited and hummed a little to herself.

At first it was easier than Finnglas had dared to hope. In the thick gloom, the sense of feeling was sharpened and each weapon came strangely different to her hand. As she grasped them, testing their edges, cutting the air with them, she found that she had not forgotten everything. Slowly, seriously, she began to lay some of them aside.

This one was too long. It would have tripped her as she walked. The next so gross and heavy that she could hardly wield it, even two-handed. These swords had been made for warriors stronger than herself. But this . . . Was Manach insulting her? A sword so light it lifted like thistledown after the others. Beautifully jewelled, by the feel of it. A hilt of twisted wire that should have sparkled in a brighter light. But a thin blade as soft as butter. A lady's toy, that would scarcely have severed a foxglove stem. She cast it away.

And now the serious weapons. She tested them with both

54

hands. And the dew was not colder than the sweat on her palms. Each of these four might have been made for her. The right length. The true weight. As her hands closed round them she could feel the workmanship of a master smith. These were rarely crafted swords, such as a queen might be proud to draw.

But then she clasped one of them a little tighter. A sense of its beauty was coming through her palms. The sharp, jewelled grip. The curiously fashioned boss, like a horned animal. A pattern of studs raised and cut to flash in the sun. She tried to imagine gripping it through a day of battle.

For the first time, she spoke aloud.

'This would be a wondrous weapon to hang in a feasting hall. A queen might give it to a poet that praised her. But a sword like this is a goldsmith's pride, not a warrior's. I would sooner grasp it by the blade than the hilt!'

Now three were left. She made as if to draw them, nestled them in her grip, passed them from hand to hand. All round her the silence deepened.

The only sound was Ranvaig knitting. The click, click of her needles in the heavy darkness. And into Finnglas's mind there came a picture, of Ranvaig tossing a knife to her, of the wheeling blade, and the haft that came clean and true into her hand.

With a small, joyful laugh she tossed the weapons into the reddened air, one after the other. Two came swooping to her hand as though they knew her, and she grasped them firmly as they dropped. But one twisted ungainly, the unbalanced hilt throwing the blade towards her, so that she snatched her hand away and let it fall. It thudded into the ground and was lost in the shadows.

She held the two that were left, each balanced on one finger, perfectly weighted at the point where the sharp edge began.

And now she was beginning to panic. She explored the hilts. Each lovingly worked with polished carvings that would not catch her clothing. Three grooves fitted her fingers. Their rounded jewels were moulded to her palm. By day they would be rich and strange. They would glow with colour. She traced the soft sheen of twining gold.

Swiftly she ran a trembling finger along the blades again. It was as she thought. These were magic swords. She felt the pattern interlaced in the beaten steel. Ribbons of metal had been leaved together, heated and hammered. Then bent and burned and beaten again. Seven times those strips had been doubled and welded, till their textures were fused with a strength that was greater than iron. Only Luis the Smith knew the secret of this work.

These blades were cool, strong, sharp, with an edge that would hold through the battle. Once more she felt the interlacing patterns. There seemed to be no difference between them. And yet there must be, there must! One of these blades would mean the gift of a kingdom. The other would cost her her life.

And they were equal. In every way. She handled the hilts again. The castings were the same. There was nothing to separate them, by a single jewel. Manach had tricked her.

'Well, lady?' And in the shadows she heard the druids' robes begin to stir and rustle.

'Let me think.'

'You must choose before the moon rises. Now.'

A deeper stillness fell. Finnglas found herself listening for something. Ranvaig had stopped knitting. And in the firelight Finnglas smiled. Across the silence, she seemed to hear Ranvaig's voice again.

'*God grant that the blood of those fish be the only life you spill.*'

'You give me rich gifts, Manach. These are swords beyond a warrior's dream. But Finnglas of the Horses shall be more than a warrior. I must be queen in peace as well as war. Where are the scabbards?'

An oath burst from Manach, and he rounded on the smith.

'Is there treachery here? Show her,' he barked. 'Bring her what you have made.'

The hunchbacked smith bowed before her. She felt a cool scabbard slide over the blade and press against her left hand. Luis the smith buckled the belt round her waist. One sword was sheathed. But on her right side, nothing.

'Well?' she asked. Her voice was the only sound in the yard. 'Where is the other scabbard?'

'The one you wear holds more magic than the blade. But there is no scabbard for the sword in your right hand.'

She let go of the hilt, as though it had been twined with snakes. The weapon lay on the ground between them. In the glow of the furnace its blade seemed to pulse with a blood-red light that nothing would ever put out.

Manach picked it up and stroked it thoughtfully. In the light from the forge his eyes glittered at Finnglas.

'So, princess? Would you fight me for your father's kingdom now?'

She heard her own voice answer strangely.

'I will fight you, if I must.'

They were given bronze-bound shields. The blades flashed out. Sparks hissed in the gloom. There was the clash of steel on steel. Feet dancing on the dark earth. Swords sweeping the air.

The end came quickly, as Finnglas had known it must. Manach knocked her blade aside. She stumbled. The round shield twisted away from her body. The sword that had no sheath flew out and slashed her arm.

The crowd shrieked.

'Finnglas!' yelled Erc helplessly. The druids held him back.

Finnglas stood still, staring down at her left arm. She could feel the blood running down to her hand, black on the pale skin. She was too shocked to move. The flames from the forge flared up in the doorway. She raised her eyes and saw the dark figure of the humpbacked smith watching.

Slowly her right hand reached across and felt for the empty scabbard. For a moment, she wished she could see the beauty of its patterning. But it must serve a deeper purpose now, and quickly. Already she was growing giddy through loss of blood.

With an effort, she lifted the scabbard and laid the bronze-bound leather across the burning wound. It felt cool, welcome, pressing the edges of severed flesh together. She closed her eyes.

She became aware that the blood was no longer trickling down her arm. Her skin was drying. Under the scabbard, the wound had ceased to throb. She let the sheath fall to her side, and felt her arm.

'I am whole,' she said.

The tribe let out its breath in a long sigh of wonder.

Manach spoke grimly through the dusk.

'Yes. You chose more wisely than you knew. You have a double gift. These are blades in ten thousand. But you chose that which can heal as well as wound. If you had taken this other . . .' His fingers nursed it regretfully. 'With a single blow I should have severed your head from your neck.'

12

Finnglas bent her head over the Game of the Hunt. Erc watched her jump the white hart sideways and take another red warrior. He could not see her face, but as she reached out her arm he glimpsed the long white scar that ran from shoulder to elbow.

'I cannot bear this!' cried Erc. 'I cannot stand by, night after night, and watch you risk your life. Is there nothing we can do?'

Finnglas's hand was not quite steady as she picked up the piece and laid it with the two defeated red huntsmen.

'Perhaps there is. Oh, Ranvaig! I do not know how I can ever thank you. It was well for me when my father made you promise to stay with me. You could have had your freedom. But you stayed, and you have saved my life.'

'I was not always a slave. But I have been a daughter, and a wife, and a mother, and it is much the same. Freedom is a fine word, but an empty heart.'

'My heart is full of gratitude.' Finnglas jumped up and flung her arms round Ranvaig. 'You taught me to choose between life and death. Twice, one of you has helped me through my trials. Niall with his homemade crot. Now you with your gutting knife.'

'But I didn't know!' Niall declared. 'I never guessed what Laidcenn would ask you to do. I only lent you my lyre to comfort you. I always sing when I'm in trouble.'

But Ranvaig looked up from the sheep's wool she was carding. Her grey eyes smiled at the princess.

'Do you not think that is why Arthmael brought us together? So that you should not have to face your trials alone. Good friends are precious. Even the little things of the earth have their uses.'

Erc sprang up, knocking the board, so that the red pieces went sliding dangerously towards the white.

'What are you saying? Do you think *I* can help Finnglas? A fisherman against wise druids and noble warriors? I don't know anything!'

'Nor I!' cried Pangur. 'I'm only good for hunting mice. And Dubhthac's not going to ask her to do that!'

'True wisdom is to be where you are needed,' said Ranvaig.

'You must have help.' Erc spoke angrily. 'But not from me. There must be someone who is wise enough to fight against Dubhthac.'

'There is one!' cried Niall suddenly. 'What a fool I've been! It is Drusticc we need now!'

'Drusticc? Who is that?'

'The Abbess of our convent, and soul-friend of us all. No, you needn't let your face fall. She is a woman, yes, and young. But straight and true as an ash tree is Drusticc. Like a sound mast to a ship, or a staff to a pilgrim. You would trust her in any storm or on any road.'

'Can she be wiser than Dubhthac? Where will I find her?'

'She is very wise. Even the birds of heaven talk with her. We left her in the Abbey a year ago. In the House of the Gulls, on the cliffs of Erin.'

'Then give me the golden ship that brought us here, Finnglas!' Erc swung round, his face glowing with hope at last. 'This at least I will do for you. Oh, I know it's a king's ship, and full of magic, and I'm a plain fisherman. But I can read the sea and the stars as well as any captain. I will use what little skill I have to fetch those who are wiser than me. Mother, pack me some food for a night and a day.'

Finnglas had risen to her feet. 'You can't leave me!' she pleaded. 'Erc, you mustn't go! I face another trial tonight. You've got to stay and help me!'

'Don't you see? It's for help I'm going. That's the only thing I can do.'

'Niall, stop him! I need him *here*!'

The big monk looked from the boy to the girl. His face was torn with doubt. Then his fist crashed down on the table, scattering the pieces on the floor.

'You're right, Erc! I'm coming with you. There are darker powers at work here than we can deal with. Drusticc alone can match Dubhthac. We *must* have help. The magic ship will take us.'

In a moment, the two of them were rushing about the house, seizing cloaks and bread and meat for the journey. Pangur fled under the table, out of their way. The two young men were almost laughing with excitement, now that they had found something they could do. Close inshore, Arthmael lifted his head out of the waves to listen.

But Ranvaig folded her arms and barred the doorway. 'You'll get no help from me. What are you thinking of? Your place is here at Finnglas's side.'

'Would you have us stand by and watch till Finnglas is dead? We'd rather risk our own lives to save her.'

'The need is here.'

'I command you, stay with me!' Finnglas cried out. 'There is no one left to help me tonight.'

'You still have Pangur Bán.'

'Me?' mewed poor Pangur from under the table. 'Erc, come back! Don't leave us alone!'

'The ship of the Golden Wolf will lend us speed. We'll be back with Drusticc before tomorrow night.'

Pushing Ranvaig aside, the two of them ran from the house, leaped into a coracle, rowed out into the harbour towards the tall ship. Pangur crawled out of hiding to watch. A golden sail began to climb the mast.

'They're weighing anchor. The sail is filling. The magic ship is on its way.'

'It's not magic we need,' said Ranvaig grimly. 'It's love and loyalty.'

Finnglas looked as if she was going to faint. She gripped the edge of the table.

'Ranvaig! What shall I do?'

Even as she spoke, the doorway darkened and the fourth summons fell at her feet. She stared down at it.

Ranvaig bent, but it was Pangur she picked up and cuddled.

'You will have to read this challenge yourself,' she told Finnglas quietly.

The princess turned the scarred rod over with shaking hands.

'Come to the hollow in the Plain of Mag Boffin, when the moon rises.'

Ranvaig watched the girl's eyes widen.

'Is that not where they lead the cattle up to summer pasture? I have heard it spoken of as a fair, broad meadow.'

'Fair is Mag Boffin, even in the driest summer, for there are streams that flow down from the mountains and water it. But all those waters drain into the hollow. It is that which has the evil name. Under the heart of Mag Boffin lies the Raven's Marsh. Why would they summon me there?

'Pangur,' she whispered. 'You are the only one I have left now. *Help me!*'

'But I don't know *how!*' squeaked the terrified white cat.

13

Erc laid his hand on the golden wolf's-head prow. The wind whipped colour into his freckled cheeks and his eyes were sparkling. This was better. Less happily, Niall ran up the gold silk sail.

'Take us to the Abbess Drusticc, in the House of the Gulls,' Erc's command rang out. And the ship leaped away from her mooring like an unleashed hound that knows its master's bidding.

At the harbour mouth, the ship swung east. The wind caught them and drove them forward. The seas ran cold and mane-tossed, chasing them. Niall set the sail square and lashed it firm. He began to relax.

Presently he looked over the side. A blue-black fin was cutting through the waves.

'It's Arthmael!' he cried. 'He's coming with us.'

Even as he spoke, the dolphin drove across their bows.

'Look out!' called Erc, swinging the helm sharply.

The dolphin threw them no look of apology or laughter. This was not the Arthmael they knew. He stormed ahead. Soon he swung round in a flurry of foam and surged back across their path.

'What's he doing?' Erc shouted, altering course angrily at the last moment. 'Does he want us to run him down? Hasn't he got enough scars already?'

Niall's hands began to hover over the knots that lashed the sheets. He glanced back at the dwindling line of grey that was the Summer Land.

'What's the matter, Arthmael? What are you trying to tell us?'

But the dolphin's face would not turn to smile at him. He was not the Clown, the Dancer, but an angry pilot, zig-zagging across their bows. With a sigh of impatience, Erc steered past him for the fourth time.

'I think we're going the wrong way,' Niall said unhappily.

'How can it be the wrong way? I told the wolfhead to take us to the House of the Gulls. Has the ship's magic ever failed us? Erin is east. You can feel the wind. It's hard from the west. We should make landfall by dawn.'

Niall looked down at the boiling wake of Arthmael. The great black flukes of a tail threshed the water as he passed. Niall groaned.

'We were wrong. The next trial is tonight. And we have left Finnglas to face it alone.'

'She is not alone. She has my mother and Pangur.'

'But it was you she wanted. You should not have left her.'

The gale fanned Erc's red hair up into flames. His eyes sparkled with anger.

'Can't you see? It's for Finnglas I'm going! I've got to get help for her, or she will die,' he shouted.

'But without you, she may die tonight!' Niall yelled at him.

Arthmael raced before beside them furiously. As the wind strengthened he dived under the ship.

They held their breath, watching for him to appear on the other side. They braced themselves for the lurch and roll if he rose under the keel. But there was nothing. The moments passed, and lengthened. They scanned the heaving sea on every side.

'I think he's gone,' said Niall uneasily. 'Erc, turn the ship. There's something very wrong.'

The boy looked back over the stern. 'Have you seen what's behind us? I couldn't change course now, if I wanted to. And I'm not going to.'

Niall turned into the west, and the coming storm whipped the cowl back from his broad shoulders. The sun was dying. A lurid yellow light lit half the sky. Beneath it, a huge cloud, black as Arthmael's head, filled the horizon, reared up out of the sea, came sweeping towards them.

Niall fell silent, gazing over their rushing wake into that wall of darkness. A deep, cold dread filled his heart.

14

The edge of the storm passed over Rath Daran. The wind howled under the thatch of Finnglas's house and the rain drummed against the walls. Then it passed, and the earth gleamed wet in the chill, grey twilight.

Pangur crouched by the fire, shivering. 'It's no use,' he mewed. 'I'm only a very small cat. What good am I to Finnglas? If only Erc had stayed.'

Ranvaig lifted him on to her knee and stroked him soothingly.

'Ssh! Don't be afraid. Anyone would think it was your life that hung by a thread, and not Finnglas's.'

'I wish it was! No, that's not true. But it's all right for you and Niall. You have done your part. What if I am the one to fail? How can I live with myself if Finnglas dies?'

The firm hands smoothed his back, over and over.

'Have courage, little cat. Arthmael chose you. He must have had a reason. When the time comes, you will know what it is. Be sure there is something you can do.'

It was dark and moonless when Finnglas rode out to the plain of Mag Boffin. Ranvaig followed, wrapped in a heavy cloak, and Pangur picked his way through the damp grass. There were shadows behind them, the spurt of torches in the creeping mist, a subdued murmur. But the crowd was smaller now. It was more than bed and a dry roof that kept many at home. There was a fear of the place by night. It was not only the streams that disappeared into the Raven's Marsh. Many the cows and cowherds that had been swallowed up under the sucking peat-bog.

The pastures were strangely silent in the night-time. No cattle lowed to them. The way was sloping downhill. Sailte's hooves splashed slightly. The ground underfoot was growing softer. Unexpectedly there came the whicker of horses and the creak of leather and wood. There were people ahead.

Finnglas reined Cloud-Clearer to a halt. Pangur crouched behind them, feeling small and frightened. Then the moon crept over the ridge and a sigh breathed from the crowd as the level silver rays lit up the scene.

The grassy meadows shone white, the turf still short after winter, ringed by dark hills against the starry night. In their hollow shone a lake of diamonds, a thousand jewelled facets of water under the gaze of the moon. The peat bog of the cattle plain, the Raven's Marsh. And rising out of it, like a fairy stronghold, a black islet of turf and rock.

On the edge of the marsh the druids were gathered, and Kernac's warriors too, with their horses and chariots.

From the island a young man's voice echoed mockingly.

'Well, Finnglas of the Horses. So my cousin has come. But not far enough. You who would be the Way-Finder of this people, can you drive a team across the Raven's Marsh? Dare you come where Rohan of the Chariots stands? There is a way to the island, but no human eye can see it. Few there are that have learned it. Others have tried to find the path, and the bog has claimed them all. Yet I have crossed it in the dark. Do you claim that you will make a braver leader than I?'

Pangur saw Rohan silhouetted against the star-filled pools. The moon caught the bronze mountings of his chariot, the flurry of his horses' manes beside him, the flash of armour.

Finnglas dismounted and walked down to the brink of the marsh. In front of her were tufts of rushes, dark patches of peat, hollows of water that might or might not have been the prints of horses' hooves. Even by daylight there was no path across the bog that eye could see.

She turned. Tomméné was leading a pair of fine ponies down the slope, drawing a chariot that shone fit for a queen.

'You send me richly to my death,' she murmured, seeing the jewelled harness, the gilded shafts, the goldsmith's work that framed the chariot. Then Pangur heard her breath catch as the moon fell full on the horses.

'I know you two, don't I?'

The golden ponies nodded their pale manes and pawed their white feet as they answered together.

'Yes! You know us. You refused to part us, Meriel from

Seiriol. And for that we are grateful to you and would serve you if we could.'

She fondled their necks gladly. 'Oh, Meriel, Seiriol! Beautiful you are. Do you know the way across the Raven's Marsh? Could you take me safely?'

They shook their heads. Their glossy skin twitched and trembled.

'We do not know the way. And we are afraid.'

Finnglas bowed her head in Meriel's mane and sighed. 'Then must I drive you to your deaths? Is there no other way? I do not want the kingdom. I would turn back from this challenge and save your lives. But Arthmael sent me for this, and I must not fail him. If I am not queen, it will be Dubhthac's power that rules the Summer Land. Yet until now it was only my own death I feared. Must I take you with me?'

A large tear fell on to Pangur's whiskers. He crept to the water's edge. He stopped suddenly. There, under his nose, was the mark of a wheel. Before he had time to think, he heard his own voice.

'Miaow!'

Finnglas lifted her head sharply. No one else had heard. The white cat's heart was beating so fiercely it almost choked him. Trembling, he stepped out on to the first clump of bulrushes growing in the bog.

He turned to stare at Finnglas. No word passed between them. Just two huge green eyes in the darkness. A glimmer of white fur, like thistledown. She understood.

She mounted up into the chariot and slapped the reins. She urged her trembling team down the grassy bank. Her eyes were fixed on Pangur, moving ahead of her like a will-o'-the-wisp in a witch's tale. She trusted her life to him.

He took a second leap, nostrils questing, finding the lingering smell of Rohan's horses, the sharp-cut edge of a hoof-print, a scraped stone. He moved out over the marsh. Belly low, as only a cat can creep. Eyes wide in the gloom, where only a cat can see. Nostrils wide to catch the scents that only a cat can smell. He went as fast as he dared, and Finnglas followed him. The crowd hardly breathed as they watched her chariot wind its way through the moonlit reeds.

Pangur knew he must not stop. He fled the fears that hunted him. What if he made just one false leap? What if the ground that bore his light body safely gave way beneath the weight of the horses and Finnglas? What if the path ended, here in the watery witchlight of the marsh, between shore and islet? The mud plopped and bubbled as he glided past. He must not pause to think.

Behind him he heard the thud and splatter of the horses' hooves and the scrape of chariot wheels on hidden stone. Finnglas's voice murmured steadily, as she calmed and coaxed her team. His green eyes darted to left and right. But Finnglas kept her gaze on that wisp of white fur. She would not let herself look at the bog on every side. If she failed, they would not need to tell her how she would die.

Without warning, Pangur stopped dead. Finnglas reined in the ponies sharply. All round them the water spread in a shining lake. No foothold of peat or mud. No craggy stones. Not even a clump of bulrushes broke the silent sheen. Pangur stared with wide eyes, terrified.

'I cannot tell which way to go!'

Hoofprints, wheelruts, had vanished under the surface. All scents had gone. The star-filled water mocked him. And just a little way beyond, the island loomed, black, firm, dangerously near. Rohan, glinting like a spear in the moonlight, came strolling down to the water's edge, on their right.

His voice jested across the water.

'Well, Finnglas of the Horses? Have you lost your courage? Will you not dare the last few steps to join me?'

The lake lay bright as a blade of steel held to the throat. But under it, to one side or the other, lurked a death that would not be swift and merciful. Finnglas gazed across the glittering strip of water at Rohan, on their right, beckoning her to him.

All the hunter's cunning woke in her. She cried suddenly, 'Pangur! Jump in! I know now which way the path lies.'

She gave a wild yell, and the reins cracked hard on the horses' rumps. The chariot turned sharply to the left. As the wheels spun past him, Pangur leaped for safety beside her.

A wave of water was flung high into the air, drowning the

stars. But the iron-clad wheels were scraping over rock. They jolted forward. The island rose in front of the straining ponies. Then the chariot gave a sickening lurch, began to topple, and stuck fast.

A wave of horror shuddered through Pangur. He waited for the wheels to begin to sink, for the terrified horses to thrash and neigh as the mud embraced them. For the silver manes and the gilded chariot to disappear from sight. For them all to go down for ever under the Raven's Marsh.

There was a distant groan from the crowd and a scream from the bursting lungs of the ponies.

Finnglas's shout rang out for the last time.

'On, Meriel! On, Seiriol! Up, my beauties!'

The mud sucked around them. The harness strained and creaked. Grinding and gurgling, the chariot rose up out of the bog, and rumbled on to the hard shore of the rocky island.

Finnglas reached out a hand and found Pangur beside her.

'A thousand thanks!' she breathed. 'Lucky was I when Arthmael gave me such counsellors.'

She stepped down from the chariot. And if her knees were shaking, she held her voice steady.

'Greetings, Rohan of the Bright Chariots.'

There was a chill silence. Then Rohan laughed without mirth.

'They named you well, Finnglas of the Horses. It seems you have won your chariot. I cannot say I am truly sorry. It would have been a crime to have drowned such a team as that. There are other ways. If you should die in battle . . .'

'If I should die in battle,' said Finnglas grimly, 'I will leave you my chariot, but not my crown.'

15

Out at sea, the wind thundered in the sail. The sheets twanged, and the planks groaned as though they would split apart. The moon that lit Pangur across the marsh never rose on the ship. The wolf's-head prow buried itself in gigantic waves and lifted again only to darkness. The ship was a living, suffering beast in pain.

'Shouldn't we reef the sail before it rips?' shouted Niall, fighting against growing terror.

'There is strong magic in this ship!' Erc yelled back. 'We have to trust to the gale if we are going to save Finnglas's life. We must find the Abbess and bring her back before another night.'

'Back?' muttered Niall. 'Sail back against this?'

A breaking wave engulfed him, knocking the breath from his body. He shook himself free of the deluge, clutching wildly at the rail.

The wolf's-head climbed, slowly, laboriously up the next unseen, mountainous roller. More cold seas swilled along the deck, knee-deep. At last they felt the ship tremble and topple, rushing downhill terrifyingly. The coming roller struck mid-mast, drenching them again. They could only cling on and wait. It seemed an agonizing time before the bows lifted again.

'For God's sake, reef the sail!' gasped Niall, when he could speak again. 'Do you want to drive us to the bottom?'

'Has the wolf-ship ever failed to reach its port? Are you more afraid for your own life than for Finnglas's?'

'How can we help her if we're drowned?'

There was a howl from the gaping mouth of the wolf-prow as it dived again into the darkness. The cold weight of the next ocean roller crashed over the ship. It swept Niall's feet from under him, flung him into the stern, chilled his fingers as they gripped round slippery wood. The world seemed upside down.

At last he felt the air rush past him, and he knew they were floating again. But the ropes that bound the sail were now far out of reach.

'Erc,' he begged. 'How much more can we take? The ship is filling with water.'

'If we cannot reach Erin by dawn, I do not care what happens to us.'

Even as he spoke, the wind screamed over the stern. The clouds were torn apart. They saw the mast bend like a stalk of corn before the sickle, heard the rending of wood, glimpsed a patch of wheeling stars where the sail had been. The next wave crashed into them, buffeting them backwards, tossing them heavily like a half-blown bladder. There was a moment's stillness. They hung between one range of rollers and the next. Then the sea struck them again, spinning them broadside.

Erc plunged amidships. 'The sail! The mast! It's gone!'

In the confusion between darkness and starlight they felt the great weight of the golden sail, tumbled over the side, filling with water, capsizing the ship.

Erc fought the heeling, rolling deck, the tangle of ropes, the cascading storm-waves. Niall groped his way forward to help. Together they struggled to haul the sail on board, but still it dragged them down.

'It's no good,' gasped Niall. 'We'll have to cut it loose.'

They had no choice. Erc's knife was out. He hacked the rigging free. With a groaning slither, mast, sail and ropes rushed overboard into the blackness of the deep.

'Then good-bye, Finnglas,' Erc muttered hopelessly.

Slowly the ship righted itself. There was an ominous sucking and swilling in the hold, and the thunder of waves against wood.

'It's too late anyway. This ship has the heaviness of death,' said Niall. Then he cupped his hands and bellowed into the night. 'Arthmael! Help us!'

There was no answer, but the hiss of wind over waves. The ship rose more heavily with every breaker.

'Arthmael?' he tried again.

But there was no reply. They huddled in wet clothes, and waited wearily for the day to come.

'Why aren't you singing?' Erc asked. 'Aren't we in trouble enough?'

'What's the good? He won't answer us.'

The ship lay low in the water, like a wounded bird. Red dawn broke, and no land was in sight. Grey waves heaved past them, still driven by the wind. But they could only wallow helplessly and heavily.

'Couldn't we row?' Erc said desperately. 'There must be something we can do!'

They hauled on the oars, but the great weight of the ship defeated them. All morning they were silent, too full of bitterness to speak to each other.

At noon, Erc burst out, 'Where is Arthmael? Why didn't he come when we needed him?'

Niall's head was hidden in his cowl. 'We have come to the Three Dark Days. This was the time of Arthmael's dying. For three days he was hidden from the world. We shall not see him until the year turns to springtime.'

'Will any of us live till then?'

The ship was dying, hour by hour, as each sea swamped her. Yet the wolf's head refused to sink. It quested on into the east as though it was still struggling to follow Erc's command. The battered wood strained and creaked.

By mid-afternoon, the deck was awash. Erc seized an axe and hacked savagely at one of the benches.

'Here, save yourself if you can. I would rather die than see the moon rise on another trial.'

He threw the bench overboard and pushed Niall after it. The next wave swept him also over the side. The chill crept into his bones and he closed his eyes. But the death he sought was slow in coming. Night fell. A piece of wreckage floated under him. He felt the rough carving of the wolf's-head. The wind and waves washed them on and on.

When he opened his eyes again, the huge silver moon was climbing over him.

He groaned aloud. 'Finnglas, forgive me! How can I help you now?'

The moon shone down pitilessly. The night was brilliant with revolving stars. But one burned clear, unchanging. It had guided Erc and Finnglas through many a dangerous sea. As he waited for death, Erc fixed his gaze again on the still, true light of the Pole Star.

All day Finnglas had sat on the chill, damp stones, staring out over the heaving sea. No curving back leaped from the cresting combers. No eye twinkled through the sunless waves. No ship had appeared out of the east.

Sailte Cloud-Clearer trotted over the meadow and blew his warm breath down her neck. Finnglas put up her arm and clasped his mane.

'Oh, Sailte. Why don't they come? Why did they leave me?'

'Because they loved you. Because their hearts were warm but not wise.'

'And Arthmael hasn't danced for me all day.'

Sailte said gently, 'Today the whole earth mourns Arthmael.'

The setting sun lit Finnglas's stricken face.

'Shame on me, that I ever thought to be a queen! I have been so full of the fear of my own failure, that I had forgotten we had come to the Darkest Day, when Arthmael himself died. Must I follow him, then? Oh, Sailte, what is going to happen tonight?'

He nudged his warm bulk against her. 'Courage. You still have friends.'

Finnglas walked back to the house. Ranvaig met her in the doorway. 'It is time to be going, my lady. They tell me it is a long journey to the Hills of Seeing.'

'The Place of the Stars. When the moon stands high, I must meet Sorcha, the wisest seer of them all.'

She brushed past Pangur into the house. As she crossed the floor, she stumbled on one of the fallen red pieces underfoot. She pitched forward, and Ranvaig caught her as she fell. Finnglas stared down. The red gaming-men were all around her. The white hind had disappeared from sight.

'Is it an omen?' she whispered.

And she hid her eyes behind her hands.

The storm had washed the sky. As Finnglas stepped down from her chariot, the broad face of the moon shed its radiance over the mountain. Dew glimmered like frost around a ring of standing stones. The shape of the granite menhirs was not quite human, yet it seemed to Finnglas as if they were alive.

As her feet met the earth she felt all the strangeness of the Place of Seeing. The years of her childhood washed over her. The quiet waiting, the patient watchfulness, eyes turned to heaven, with the cold eating slowly into a body that had become quite unimportant. In the House of the Stars, life had turned on the wheels of the astronomer's mind.

Sorcha Clear-Sight was standing in the circle. Few there were that had climbed this far to watch the fifth trial, up the long road into the star-hung mountains. Silent druids, bards humming as though the wind swept through hanging harps, the warriors nervous, shifting their feet on hallowed ground. It was not distance alone that had kept the common people away. The Place of Seeing was a threshold to other worlds, dangerous in darkness.

There were watchful shadows behind the shadowy stones.

'Come,' Sorcha summoned Finnglas.

As she took a step forward, the earth seemed to shift beneath her feet, so that she almost cried out. There was a new strangeness here, stronger than any night she had ever known. These were the stones she remembered, but they were not as she remembered them. She cast her eyes round them wildly. There should be six tall pillars pointing to the sky, six wide boulders rooted in the ground. Swiftly she began to count. One, two, three . . . twelve, *thirteen*. Her eyes flew round the circle again. No, she had been wrong. There were only twelve. Dizzily now, as the blazing stars began to shift and sway, she numbered them for the third time. Six boulders, seven pillars. There were thirteen houses in the Wheel of the Year.

Sorcha was beckoning her into the ring.

'Are you afraid of the Seeing? The stars are for our guiding. You must stand at the axis and tell the wheel's secret, if you would be queen over all the Summer Isle. Come, Finnglas Redhand.'

She felt the barrier. This was a ring of power. Inside lay the moonlit grass where only a seer of nine years' secrets might stand. Yet Sorcha had the power to summon here whomever she named. Finnglas came to her, carefully but obediently. She thought she saw shadows stir behind the stones as she passed.

Sorcha's clear voice rang with the echoes of childhood. 'These Stones are for the stars. For the track of the Travellers up the heavenly way. For the winds that blow over our herds and speed our ships. For the constellations in their rising. So that we may count and cast and watch the dance come circling every year.'

'All this I know,' said Finnglas. But her mind was reeling as her eyes spun round the circle. Once she *had* known this, but tonight it had changed.

'Then your task will be easy.' Was that laughter in Sorcha's voice? 'If you know the twelve ports of the Goddess, you will recognize the pilot of the Queen. Only the one who can tell that, is fit helmsman to steer this tribe.'

The moon watched as the silence lengthened. Pangur felt the fur prickle along his spine. They said these stones danced when no human was watching. Finnglas was turning slowly round the circle.

Surely these Stones of Seeing could not have moved? Yet there were thirteen menhirs now. Twelve she had known. Which one was the stranger?

It seemed an age to the watchers. Only Sorcha stood tall and still. Finnglas lifted her face to the star-filled sky. If only she could escape from her body now. Be carried up, far out of danger. Such things were possible to the druids.

The cold sank into her bones. The face of the moon stared full into her face. She felt as if she were drowning in an icy sea.

'Erc!' she cried out. 'Erc, where are you?'

And all of a sudden, she was in another time. She was riding the swaying deck of the golden ship. The winter night was bitter around her. She and Erc, wrapped in their fur cloaks, were battling with the steering oar as the ship flew south past the coasts of Erin. While the others lay dreaming of home,

Finnglas and Erc had challenged each other to star-lore, calling each constellation glimpsed between hurtling clouds. But as waves and wind rose blacker and higher, they had looked grimly over their shoulders and held their course by the one True Star.

The watchers heard her laugh aloud. She began to fly round the circle, striking each stone as she sped past and shouting aloud to the stars.

'I name the House of the Water-Bearer, the Fishes, the Lamb.

'The House of the Bull, the Two-fold Child, the Ship . . .'

The shadows started, and the menhirs began to sway.

'Have a care of the Stones!' cried Sorcha, her voice suddenly urgent.

Still Finnglas ran and sang out,

'The House of the Lion, the Virgin, the Balanced Scales.

'The Serpent, the Centaur, and the Goat from the Sea.

'And here!' She flung her arms round the northernmost stone at last and laughed breathlessly. 'Thanks to Erc's lessons! This thirteenth stone is not a stranger but a friend. The Pole Star points to the only true stone for a queen. Let your changing ones dance through the circling seasons. I name the Unchanging One to be my guide.'

As she clung to the stone there came a deafening roar all around her. The earth leaped beneath her feet as twelve great granite menhirs came crashing inwards, flattening everything beneath them.

Finnglas let out a cry of terror. The moon flashed suddenly brilliant over the shadowless hilltop. The earth groaned with its wound. Everywhere high druids and nobles were prostrate on their faces around the circle, struck down by awe.

As Finnglas looked wildly up, she thought the stars themselves were falling on her. The stone above her too seemed to lean, to topple. With a scream she let go. She leaped from the circle, jumping fallen menhirs, praying druids. Stumbling, running. Voices called her name as she passed, but her ears were deaf with the blood that was hammering in them. She plunged blindly, wildly down the hill to the Forest and threw herself into the sheltering arms of the trees.

She did not see that, behind her on the mountain-top, the one great pillar she had embraced still stood unshaken, with all the others on their faces before it. The druids were rising to their feet.

Only Sorcha stood calmly, unmoved as the Queen-Stone she had set. Her laughter greeted them.

'What did I tell you?' she asked. 'You see? She has forgotten nothing. And she has learned a wisdom I could not teach.'

But Pangur was already bounding down the hill after Finnglas, with Ranvaig hurrying behind. They stopped on the edge of the forest, where the moonlight ended.

'Finnglas?' called Pangur into the darkness.

The oaks whispered together.

'Oh, Ranvaig,' wailed Pangur. 'Where has she gone?'

They looked at each other fearfully. Ranvaig's eyes were hollows of darkness. Pangur's glittered green. Not a word was spoken between them, but reluctantly they turned and took the first step into the whispering forest.

'Finnglas?' they called softly as they went.

'Ssh,' muttered the oak leaves over their heads.

Ranvaig gave a little gasp as brambles clawed at her shawl. Pangur crept wide-eyed along the deer-path. His whiskers bristled with the scent of danger.

'Finnglas?' he mewed. But his voice was beginning to shake with the thought of what might live in the heart of this forest.

Suddenly he stopped in his tracks.

'What is it?' whispered Ranvaig, almost falling over him.

'Listen!' hissed Pangur.

There was only the faint breath of the night wind in the treetops. But in his mind there echoed the crack of a twig. They waited in the quiet that was not quite silence. The wood was full of rustlings. At last Pangur moved on.

The way was leading down the hill, through the soft shuffle of last year's leaves. Pangur's ears were tensed to listen and his blood ran chill with the thought of pole-cats and wolves. He tried not to think of something worse.

'Hsst!' Again he checked abruptly.

Ranvaig put up a hand and pushed away a hanging creeper. It creaked against the tree-trunk above her head. When it stopped there was no other sound. But in Pangur's ears there echoed the thud of a footfall.

They went on again, in silence, close together. Below them now they could hear the murmur of a brook over stones.

Ranvaig called out suddenly, making Pangur almost jump out of his skin with fright.

'Finnglas!' Her voice went ringing through the forest.

The cat strained to listen. The echoes wandered away through the unseen trees, leaving a deeper stillness. Only the brook chuckled in the dark valley.

'It's no good. We've lost her,' said Pangur. 'She could be . . . Yeeow!'

Ranvaig screamed out too. Hands seized her from behind. Faces panted all around her. Something had grabbed Pangur and scooped him into the air. He fought and scratched and twisted. A man's oath rang out.

'Pest! Kill him!'

A knife hissed from its sheath. With a great leap Pangur sprang free and dived for safety under a bramble bush.

'The devil! I've lost him. Whatever he is, he's got claws like dragon's teeth.'

'You fool! Don't let him escape. He'll bring death on us.'

'He's in these bushes here.'

There was a trampling all round him. Sticks beat down the covering leaves. Pangur crouched trembling, too scared to move. Another sharp branch came stabbing towards him. It struck him bruisingly. He clenched his teeth, willing himself not to cry out.

At last, muttering and swearing, the strangers gathered on the path.

'He's gone, drat him.'

'And knows too much.'

'That's the second one tonight. What's going on?'

'We should have let them pass by, like the other.'

'This pair came too close. They'd have stumbled on us anyway.'

'We've still got one of them.'

'Then kill her now, and make sure of her.'

'No. Not till we learn what their game is. Take her to Liudhard. Then we'll silence her tongue.'

'You. March!'

They jostled Ranvaig down the path. Her hands were bound. Since the first cry, she had not spoken a word. But her head kept turning from side to side, as if she was listening to her captors curiously.

Pangur held his breath and heard them pass by, till their

voices were drowned in the murmur of the brook. Then he crept back on to the path. For a moment, he stood alone, wondering. Far, far above him were the druids on the hilltop, plotting the sixth trial. And somewhere, stumbling in the vast tracts of the forest, Finnglas was lost and afraid. Erc and Niall had vanished on the storm, beyond recall. And below, Ranvaig was now a prisoner in great danger.

'Arthmael!' he mewed helplessly. 'What shall I do?'

The trees moaned and seemed to press closer around him. He had never felt so far from the sea and the loving dolphin. But he did not need the words in his ear to tell him where he must go.

'At least, they were only men!' he told himself.

Plucking up all his courage, he set off down the path behind Ranvaig.

The ground fell sharply away in front of Pangur. A grassy hollow beside the brook was brilliant with moonlight. It was studded with shelters made of bent branches. On the white grass between them, a fire had been smothered with turf.

An angry buzz rose through the trees to Pangur. Shadowy creatures were crawling out of the shelters, seizing branches, clubs, knives with glittering blades. Ranvaig stood upright among her captors, a still, small figure, with her hands bound. The creatures swarmed round her.

Pangur crept nearer down the bank. He stole out into the edge of the moonlight, a white ghost on the pale grass, and crouched to listen.

'We caught her hardly a sling-cast from the camp.'

'There are more of them in the woods. We heard them calling to each other.'

'Better to have left them alone, then. Fools! Do you want to bring all Kernac's spearmen on our hiding-place?'

'There was an animal with her. Vicious as a dragon. He got away. And took the skin of my hands with him.'

'You let one of them escape? He'll bring death to all of us.'

Ranvaig's voice rose above the hubbub.

'Death? That is the white cat that set you free, when you were slaves in Kernac's kitchen. If you can call this freedom. Hiding in the forest. Afraid of every footfall in the grass.'

There was a startled silence. Then clamour broke out around her, louder than ever.

'Who are you?'

'How do you know us?'

'Who told you about the fire in Kernac's kitchen?'

Ranvaig's teeth smiled in the moonlight.

'I was once a slave, as you were. Don't you recognize me?'

The crowd fell back. Someone ripped a turf from the fire and pulled out a branch. It flared suddenly in the night breeze and the flame blazed red on Ranvaig's face. Then they pressed forward crying eagerly,

'Ranvaig of Senargad!'

'We thought you were dead! We saw you standing in the blazing doorway when the palace caught fire.'

'We called to you to run, but you didn't follow us.'

Ranvaig held up her hand for silence.

'The white cat, Pangur Bán, set fire to the palace and gave you freedom. But he brought me a greater gift from Senargad. My lost son, Erc. For that, I stayed. And because Kernac asked me to.'

'You mean . . . you're still Kernac's slave? You, a woman who was born free?'

'The king gave me my freedom with his dying breath. I chose to serve his daughter of my own free will.'

'Kernac is *dead*?' A wave of astonishment ran round the escaped slaves. 'Then . . . who is king in the Summer Land?'

Pangur heard his own voice, high and squeaky.

'There is no king. The Princess Finnglas claims the sceptre, in Arthmael's name. And she is in peril of her life and her reason. Help us find her.'

The crowd swung round and gasped as they saw the white cat standing under the moon. To Pangur's embarrassment, they fell down on their knees in front of him.

'It is the white cat himself!'

'Pangur Bán, our deliverer!'

'Honoured sir, what can we do to thank you?'

Pangur was glad the moonlight paled his blushing nose.

'Get up. Please. I only did what the Dolphin told me. It's Princess Finnglas who matters. The druids have put her to seven trials, on peril of death, to win the kingdom. She has passed the first five. But tonight, in the moment of victory, the darkness of death seemed to enter her soul. She has lost herself in the forest now, and we must find her.'

The crowd got to their feet, babbling excitedly. Liudhard, their leader, spoke for all of them. 'There was someone running in the forest. We thought it was a young man, and let him pass. But it could have been your princess. She crossed the stream above our camp, and went on west.' He looked up at the moon, dipping behind the trees. 'The moon is setting. She will be far off now.'

'We have to find her. Before the next moon sets she must take the sixth trial, or the kingdom will be ruled by darkness. And . . . and because she's frightened.'

'The Forest is vast, but there are many of us. If she is here, we will have news of it. We will search every bramble bush until we find her.'

Ranvaig looked steadily at Pangur.

'One of us must go back to Rath Daran. The sixth challenge comes at noon. Wait for her there, and tell Sailte what has happened.'

'But what shall I do if the challenge comes and she isn't back?' mewed Pangur. 'And even if she is, who is left to help her now?'

'While she has friends,' said Ranvaig, 'there is always hope.' But her face was grim as she turned to the slaves' leader.

'Liudhard, if you find any news of the princess, send it swiftly to the white house below Rath Daran.'

19

Hands loosed Erc's grip on the wolf-head and lifted him on board. He cried out in agony as life began to return to his numb hands and feet. He opened his eyes. Two faces were bending over him in monkish cowls, one dripping water. Niall's and a lined and worried one he did not know.

'He's alive, thanks be to God,' said Niall. 'You've saved us both, Enoch. Let's hope we're not too late to save Finnglas too.'

Erc groaned again as the pain reached his memory.

'Another trial has gone! Can she still be alive?'

'Keep your courage up, lad. Look, there's the House of the Gulls. It was Enoch, the convent fisherman, who picked us up. We'll be at the abbey now in two shakes of a cormorant's tail.'

Erc struggled to sit up in the fishing-boat. It was full morning. The waves were dashing white against tall cliffs. Small huts clung to the ledges, like flecks of spume. A high stone cross speared the sky.

Enoch, in brown woollen robes like Niall's, moved to the mast. He hoisted the reefed sail and brought the ship leaping in between lanes of rock. An islet flashed by. The sail came tumbling down. The fishing-boat lay rocking in a sheltered bay.

Niall scrambled overboard and turned to help Erc.

'You'll need dry clothes and food. This was no weather to be at sea,' said Enoch, as they supported the boy up the beach. 'Brogan!'

Another monk came running down the cliff path.

'It's the Abbess we need,' said Niall. 'It doesn't matter about us.'

'Niall!' Brogan flung wide his arms with a welcoming smile. 'We thought you were in the Summer Isle with the princess

Finnglas. Have you came back to us? But you're soaking wet. And the boy looks half-dead.'

Shame darkened Niall's face.

'We came to fetch Drusticc to help us. And we may have done great wrong. Arthmael tried to warn us. But fear made us blind and deaf.'

'Our ship foundered. But we must bring help to Finnglas,' Erc cried. 'Will you lend us a boat?'

'Sail back in this wind?' Enoch shaded his wrinkled eyes and stared out to sea. 'No ship could do it. Two days this gale has been setting from the west.'

Erc, the fisherman, hung his head. 'I would not see it,' he muttered. 'Then there's no hope left.'

A silence fell over them. At last Niall said in a low voice, 'I had better find Drusticc and tell her what we have done.'

'She is where you will always find her in the Darkest Days. In her Place of Prayer,' Brogan told them. 'Can the boy make it? It's a steep climb.'

'For Finnglas I would go through fire,' Erc answered.

He dragged himself up the cliff path behind Niall. At the top was a tiny stone chapel. Erc paused gratefully. But Niall was striding on towards the mountains. Still they climbed, over rough grass and heather. Veils of cloud were blowing across the hills. Soon the fog wrapped them in a soft, cold rain.

'I can't get any wetter,' Erc shouted. 'But how will we ever see to find her in this?'

'She's a difficult woman to miss,' Niall called back to him. 'Listen.'

There was the sound of running water on their left. Niall veered towards it.

It was not, after all, hard to find Drusticc. Snatches of song came to them out of the mist.

> 'Be thou my vision, O Lord of my heart.
> Naught be all else to me save that thou art.
> Thou my best thought by day or by night,
> Waking or sleeping, thy presence my light.'

'Over here,' called Niall, splashing through tussocks of bog grass.

The Abbess was singing at the top of her voice.

> 'Be thou my battle-shield, sword for the fight,
> Be thou my dignity, thou my delight . . .'

She was standing up to her waist in the middle of a peat stream. The gale flapped the white wool of her robes around her body. Her face was lifted to welcome the beating rain. She saw Niall and Erc and waved cheerfully to them.

'What's the matter with you, lads? Have you forgotten how to sing when you're in trouble?'

Niall joined his voice to hers.

> '. . .Thou my soul's shelter, thou my high tower.
> Raise thou me heavenward, O Power of my power.'

She stood unmoved in the wind and the wet, singing lustily to the end of the verse. When she had finished, she stepped out on to the bank and wrung the water from her skirt. Her face was still young, but her hair was white. Her bare feet were purple with cold, which she seemed not to notice.

'For the love of Michael, what would you two be doing in Erin? Is Finnglas queen of the Summer Isle already?'

'We don't even know if she's still alive,' Niall burst out. 'We wanted to help her. But it's all gone wrong!'

She turned a piercing look upon the boy.

'You'll be Erc, I suppose? The gulls told me of you. But what in the world are you doing here when Finnglas needs you?'

'It's for her we came! The druids have challenged her to seven trials, on peril of death. There were only four of us. We had to fetch you. I couldn't help her. How can I fight against nobles and druids?'

'The gulls speak of you as a great nobleman.'

'I'm only the poor son of a fisherman!'

'In the House of the Gulls, there are kings' sons who serve in the kitchen, and slaves who order their work. Those who act nobly are noblemen and women here. Once you saved many lives, at great cost to yourself. Why have you left her alone now?'

'To fetch *you*!'

'By the staff of Patrick, but you two are a pair of fools! Did you think Arthmael would not have given her all the help she needed? Why do you think he sent you with Finnglas? Even Pangur has more sense than that. It was *you* she wanted in her hour of need, not me.'

'Then, could she . . . will she die *because* of us?'

'I should have guessed.' Niall bowed his head. 'We've been idiots.'

Drusticc's face softened as she looked at them. 'She owes her life to you already, and more than her life. Take courage, lads! Arthmael is not called the World's Fool for nothing. He has a way of using even idiots, praise be. Quick now, back to the convent with you, for dry clothes and a bowl of soup. We must be off within the hour.'

'But how . . .'

The Abbess was already striding ahead of them, down through the heather into the wind, dripping water as she went. As they came out of the mist, the wild white wave-caps were still dashing past the bay. Niall caught up with her.

'But our ship is wrecked. We can't get back to the Summer Isle. What could sail against this wind?'

Drusticc swung round. An old mischief sparkled in her eyes.

'There are more ways than water to the Summer Land. How do you think Kernac's army came upon us so suddenly three years ago? Did you never hear of the Causeway of Lir?'

Niall stared at her. 'Yes,' he said warily. 'And of the sea that rolls over it at the flood. They say it is too long for human foot to cross between tide and tide.'

'Then we must ask for fleeter legs.'

Drusticc whistled piercingly. From the misty hills behind them came a low thrumming. Then a galloping, growing, drumming, faster, coming. Down through the heather in a wave of scattered raindrops swept two tall, antlered stags. They wheeled before the Abbess, red-coated, with quick black eyes and restless hooves.

'Gently, my beauties. Whoa, Furbaide; steady, Feradach. Greetings to you.'

Her hands soothed them. They hung their crowned heads and nuzzled her palms. She stood between them, one white-clad arm over each proud red neck.

'Listen, my darlings. There is work to do for the swiftest feet and the boldest hearts. For the love of Arthmael, would you lend us your speed and courage? Will you race the moon and the tide? Do you consent to come under my yoke?'

Their deep voices bayed. 'For Arthmael's name, we will do it. For a night and a day our speed and our strength are yours.'

Drusticc's white teeth laughed out of her wind-burned face at the two young men.

'So!' she cried. 'Now you shall see how a nun can drive a chariot!'

20

The hearth of the white house was cold. The gaming pieces were tumbled on the floor. Pangur Bán leaped in through the window. The empty house had the feel of fear and desolation.

It must be almost noon. But the sun was hidden. Clouds were thickening across the April sky. Too soon he heard footsteps outside. Though he had been expecting them, his ears pricked and flattened. This was not the swift running of Alprann, the royal messenger. They were the footsteps of men, heavy with authority, three of them. They stopped outside the closed door.

Dubhthac the druid laughed long and low.

'So she has not returned! The game is mine. We have broken the spirit of Finnglas Redhand.'

Tomméné's voice cut angrily across his. 'Finnglas, daughter of Kernac, is no coward! By the gods, if you were not a druid, Dubhthac Golden-Knife. . .'

'It wants many hours to the setting of the moon. The game is not lost or won yet.' It was Manach, the weapon-master, shrewdly weighing how this might work to his advantage.

'I say she has failed. There is no one here to receive the challenge. Even her low-born friends have deserted her.'

'Miaow!' called Pangur indignantly from inside the house.

There was a moment's silence. Then Manach laughed.

'It's only the cat! Come, Dubhthac, you are right. We must seek a ruler somewhere else.'

'Rubbish!' Pangur sprang out through the window and stood defiantly before them, back arched and fur bristling in spikes. 'Only the cat, is it? Who was it swam from Iona with the Dolphin and rode the wild-sea horses of Manawydan? Who was it rescued Finnglas from the tower of Jarlath of the Wolves? Or who set fire to the palace of Kernac the king? I am Pangur Bán!'

Tomméné roared with amusement. 'You're a bold puss! I can see why Finnglas would choose you for her friend. But where is the princess, Pangur? This challenge is for her hand.'

'You may trust it to me, Tomméné mac Ruain. It shall reach Finnglas of the Horses before moonrise tonight.'

He spoke more bravely then he felt. Dubhthac the druid smiled slow and cruelly. 'You must find her first. It seems that Finnglas Redhand cannot face another trial.'

Pangur snarled at him. 'I dare you to say that to her face and see what happens! Finnglas has taken five trials and passed them. She will not fail the sixth.'

'Then bid her enter the cave of Gormgall the Fair, when the moon goes down.'

And with a low chuckle at Pangur's face he dropped the red-stained alder rod at his feet. Then he turned and strode back to Rath Daran, with the two warriors following uneasily behind him.

Pangur stood looking at the message, not daring to touch it. His eyes went longingly to the grey troubled sea. It was as cold and empty as the clouded sky.

'Oh, Arthmael, where *is* Finnglas?' he wailed aloud. 'And what's become of Niall and Erc? Is there nobody left but me?'

There was a trampling of hooves, and chestnut Sailte came galloping up from the beach, whinnying.

'Pangur Bán! Is Finnglas with you? I was so worried when you didn't come back last night. Is Finnglas safe?' There was fear in the horse's dark eyes.

'Finnglas is lost,' Pangur answered shortly.

'But she is still alive?' Sailte begged. 'Tell me that Finnglas did not fail the trial!'

'She is somewhere in the Great Forest. But the next challenge has come. The day is more than half gone, and I don't know where I am to find her . . . Or if she wants to be found.'

'Look, what's that?' neighed Sailte.

A man was running out of the woods towards them, crouched low and looking cautiously to left and right.

'It's one of the runaway slaves!' Pangur bounded to meet him. 'Tell us quickly, Liudhard! Is there news of Finnglas?'

21

Niall and Erc clung to the sides of the jolting, leaping, bucketing chariot. The stags flew across the mountainside as if they had wings. Sparks shot from their slender hooves in the dying light. Night fell and they went careering through the darkness. Beside them Drusticc's white robe glimmered. Her hood streamed out behind her and her voice called fiercely to her team.

'On, my beauties; on, my little brothers!'

The moon rose and they were bowling over sloping meadows in a wide white wonder of a world and the scent of crushed spring flowers. Niall gripped the wickerwork as the silver disc climbed like a slow slingshot through the stars to stand overhead. He watched it arch towards its setting. Words were torn from him painfully.

'The sixth trial. And where is Finnglas now? May Arthmael send her help!'

Together Erc and he saw the moon go down behind the mountains. Still Drusticc cried, 'On, Furbaide! On, Feradach!'

The sky was paling to the seventh day and the first glimmer of the sea lay in the west. On through the level farmlands and the blossoming apple orchards. On to the rocky coast and the long white sands. On into a jewelled dawn that gilded all the rocks in a sapphire sea.

Far out in the west, across a wide and sparkling sound, the green mountains of the Summer Isle stood caught in the sunrise. A rocky causeway stretched like a pointing finger from the shore. But the wind was still driving hard from the west and white wave crests flashed over the stones and fell back with hungry sighs. The tide was dropping.

Hexagonal rocks, like cells in a honeycomb, honey-gold where the sun fell on them, rose into the light. But where the waves still washed, they were green with weed and brown with slime and black with danger.

'On, my darlings! On, my little angels!'

Drusticc leaned over the reins urgently. Before the stone spine had risen clear of the sea, the wicker chariot went vaulting out on to the Causeway. The bounding wheels ground the limpet shells into dust, sliced through the dulse, exploded the bladderwrack. Watchful waves reared up beside them and fell back again with a slap. The powerful red necks of the stags strained against the harness.

'On, my jewels! On, my cherubim!'

The chariot was slipping from side to side on the wet rocks, jumping across the cracks between the stones. The stags were flying towards the Summer Isle too swift for safety and too fast to fall.

'On, brave hearts!'

They were halfway across the Causeway when the tide turned. Niall glanced behind him and caught his breath. The light of morning glittered across the whole length and breadth of the wind-tossed sound. They were as far from the shores of Erin as from the distant Isle. He looked down into the clear depths. The waves were splashing through the spokes of the wheels.

Niall caught Erc's eye, but they did not speak. They watched the waves writhe up the sides of the rocks like climbing serpents. The first breaker splashed Niall in the chariot seat.

'On!' muttered Drusticc. 'On, for the love of Jesus!'

The stags lunged and leaped. Spray whitened their antlers and darkened their hides. The long sands of the Summer Isle seemed to swim towards them through the flying foam with the slowness of a dream. The waves were rising all around them, smooth-faced, but angry-crested. And all the time, the golden causeway was sinking, sinking down into the sea. The flooding tide rushed in and drowned it.

With a ringing yell, Drusticc let go of the reins. The stags, released, sprang forward even more swiftly. The stones were hidden, yet they flew across them, straight and true as two flung spears through a salmon pool. Waves burst on the rocks and the wheels threw them back again. The air was hissing with spray.

And still the sea was rising, over the spokes, over the hubs, to the chariot floor.

Two breakers reared, higher than all the rest. Pillars of emerald swaying over their heads, towering, toppling. Drusticc seized her staff and brandished it above her.

'By the name of the Father, the Son and the Living Spirit!'

In the green darkness the staff blazed with a silver brilliance. An unseen strength seemed to force the watery walls apart. The hanging foam trembled.

'*On*, Furbaide! *On*, Feradach!'

Into the tunnel of climbing combers they plunged. The sky disappeared. There was only the rush of the wheels through water, the rattle of hooves on stone, and the red stags' powerful panting breath.

'On,' muttered Drusticc. 'On, for mercy's sake!'

She held her arm high overhead. The arching breakers whispered devouringly. On the ends of the shining staff time hung suspended.

The wave-crests cursed and curled. Niall saw her arm begin to shudder. In an instant he flung himself forward, supporting her hands.

The staff burned more fiercely.

'My thanks,' she murmured. ''Twould be a pity if Finnglas lived and we were drowned!'

At the end of the tunnel light was growing from green to gold. Niall's arm was growing weary too. The wave-walls were starting to break. But the Causeway was rising under their wheels, lifting the spokes from the sea. Sparks were flying on every side from sun-kissed rocks, and the sky was cloudlessly blue over them, and all the gulls were shouting for joy.

Drusticc lowered her staff at last with a shaking arm.

'Whoa, my princelings. That was nobly done. Will you look there?'

Behind them broke a mighty roar. The cheated waves flung themselves in fury over the Causeway, smothering it, obliterating it, burying it deep beneath a press of tumbled waters.

'Now to the three-fold Name, a thousand blessings,' gasped Drusticc, wiping the spray from her face.

The stags hung their great heads, gulping in sweet air. Their flanks heaved, and their slender knees quivered. Their red coats steamed in the sun.

Still speechless, Erc and Niall stepped down from the chariot and stroked the beasts' sides gratefully. The strong breeze danced around them. Gulls screamed overhead. They saw the seas run full and deep over the path where they had driven.

'Well?' asked Drusticc. 'Did you bring me here to sit on the beach and watch the tide come in?'

'Finnglas!' The colour left Erc's face. 'We've been away three nights. What may have happened to her?'

Niall fondled the faces of the stags earnestly. 'Noble brothers. You have served us more generously than we deserved. Have you strength enough left to carry us to Rath Daran?'

Furbaide and Feradach tossed their antlers to the sun. Their eyes gleamed proudly. 'For a night and a day our speed is yours to command. Did we not give you our word?'

Drusticc reined in her team as they came in sight of the white house at Rath Daran. No smoke rose from the thatch. The door was closed. It was the noon of the seventh day.

Niall and Erc leaped down from the chariot and ran towards the house, calling anxiously.

'Finnglas! Finnglas! Are you there!'

A small white cat uncurled itself from the threshold and sprang to meet them.

'Niall! Erc! Is it really you at last? Oh, why didn't you come back in time?'

22

Terror imprisoned Finnglas. She did not see the Queen Stone still standing unmoved where she had hugged it. She did not feel Ranvaig's hands catch at her as she tore past. She did not hear Pangur's cry behind her. She fled from the Place of Seeing. On she raced down the hill, in the blinding, brilliant moonlight, till the deep woods stretched out their arms to receive her, and she hid herself under their darkness.

Still she ran, sobbing and stumbling. The moonlight was treacherous in the forest. Pools of light promised open clearings and did not show her the brambles that barred the way. Shadows lay like solid branches across the path, driving her needlessly into the undergrowth. She was scratched and torn, fighting the foliage with tear-filled eyes. She scarcely knew what she was doing or where she was going. White owls swooped soundlessly across her path, and the woods were full of rustlings and small screams.

Fear drove her. Worse than the fear of darkness or the fear of death. The fear of failure.

'Arthmael! Help me!' she called.

But how could the Dolphin come to her, here in the forest?

She did not see the stone that catapulted into the oak above her head. She did not sense the escaped slaves whispering urgently around her path. She did not hear Pangur and Ranvaig calling to her in the far distance. She rushed on, beyond feeling, beyond knowing, hearing only the terror in her heart.

The night aged, and the shadows turned from black to grey. At last a great weariness began to overcome her. Her overburdened mind longed to rest, to shut out the past in sleep, to hide from the future. Her chest was heaving, and her knees were beginning to buckle and sway.

'Arthmael,' she moaned again.

95

There was a rustling in the bushes on her right. This time she heard it. She lifted her head and looked to one side. It was just beginning to get light under the trees. There was a flicker of ghostly white, and then nothing. Only the sound of thudding footsteps, that might or might not be her own. The path forked and thankfully she veered left.

The next warning was a low growl behind her, to her other side. Finnglas was startled now. Her hand flew to her belt. But there had been no place for her new sword in the House of the Stars. Still, this was a danger she could understand. She began to look around her for a stout branch. A sharp crack of twigs rang closer on her left. She doubled away, and found herself running down a long ride to her right. Her feet were pounding over soft peat. She glanced behind her. The ride was empty. Her steps started to slacken as she ran on.

Then, unmistakably, the silence was shattered by a deep-throated howl. She looked round once more and her pulses raced. A great, white creature with scarlet ears was racing towards her, four-footed, yet more than half her own height, tongue panting and teeth bared eagerly.

She fled from it. She could hear its breathing gaining on her. There was a hollow of sky ahead of her at the end of the tunnel and the stars were paling with every stride. It was nearly morning. The trees flew past, then bushes, brambles. And suddenly the west lay open before her. A grassy slope, starred with hawthorn and gorse. A broad, shining river far below, that looped its way around a quiet farm. And in the distance, the ocean, flecked golden with the dawn.

A choking cry rose from Finnglas's heart.

'The House of Ana!'

Her foster-home, that had meant shelter and joy through the years of childhood. Where she had played with her brother, and learned the ways of her people, and grown into a woman and a princess.

And in that moment, all fear was forgotten. The huge spectre pursuing her, the druids plotting the next trial, the loss of Erc and Niall. She was rushing down the slope, her flying feet scarcely skimming the ground.

A long line of cattle was swinging its slow way towards the

dairy. A large woman stood in the doorway, with her hands on her hips, calling each beast by name in a singing voice that was deep and rich and loving.

'Ana!' cried Finnglas breathlessly to her foster-mother.

On the crest of the hill the great white hound paused, crowned by the rising sun. It watched the woman lift her face to Finnglas, heard her singing call float up the wind. The hound's teeth parted in a grin.

23

It was like running in a dream, with the grass thick about her ankles, and the sun warm on her shoulders and all the dawn birds singing. And then Finnglas was in amongst the cattle, feeling their steaming red rumps and breathing their sweet, rich smell.

Ana was sitting on a three-legged stool in the morning sunshine. Strong hands drew the milk hissing down into the pail. Her broad, green-gowned back was turned to Finnglas, and as she worked, she sang.

> 'Sunrise, moonwise, new and old,
> The right hand and the left,
> The waking and the dreaming self,
> The warp that needs the weft.'

She slapped the cow on the rump and it lumbered obediently away into the meadow. She called the next beast to her by its own name. As it came, Ana turned, thick brown plaits swinging against her red cheeks. Her eyes, dark as burning peat, lingered over Finnglas, enfolding her into the herd, knowing her as she knew them. But she said nothing, only started to sing again as the milk came foaming down with glad spurts.

> 'The daytime comes, the dark gives way,
> The dawn has married shade and sun.
> The sleeper's dream, the worker's day,
> In dreams are all our works begun.'

The yard was sweet with the smell of new-fallen dung and the croon of wood-pigeons in the thatch. Children wandered out of the farmhouse door, rubbing sleep from their eyes, and squatted on the grass chewing crusty bread. Finnglas sat down too, where she had watched so many mornings of her life, and waited till the herd had yielded up its milk. Ana straightened her back to her full height. She set a yoke across her wide shoulders and lifted two full pails easily. The milk swung creamily against the wood. Unbidden, Finnglas picked up the third. She followed her foster-mother across the yard. The heavy hips and the swinging plaits passed through the doorway into the cool shadows of the house. The children on the doorstep smiled at Finnglas, curious and unafraid. Finnglas found herself smiling back at them in sudden shyness as she entered.

The woman set down her pails and turned. Still she said nothing. But she gazed deep into the girl's eyes and Finnglas felt the truth drawn out of her, like a thorn from a finger. The mother's hands broke bread from a loaf. She dipped a beaker of milk, and held them out to Finnglas. Her voice was rich as the lowing of cattle.

'Come, child. Eat. Drink. In this house there is always welcome.'

Obedient as the red cows, known and loved as they were, Finnglas sat down at the table and broke her fast. As she drained the last of the rich milk, and swallowed the final crumb, her head began to sink with weariness. Ana still looked at her, and Finnglas found she could no longer hold back the tears.

'Oh, Ana!' she cried. 'For five days I've been so afraid!'

And she was on her knees before her foster-mother, her face buried in the wide lap. Firm hands caressed her shaking shoulders. The fire spurted on the hearth. The voices of the children playing echoed from the yard, with the call of the swallows. And Ana sang.

> 'The petals fade to make the fruit,
> The corn is scythed to sow,
> The fallen acorn puts out root,
> Life dies, that life may grow.'

Finnglas turned her face desperately up to Ana.

'It is not for myself! Do not think I am afraid to die. I would go gladly to a warrior's death if it would do any good. But what I fear, what I dread day and night, is that I, Finnglas of the Horses, might fail Arthmael, and there will be darkness in the Summer Land for ever!'

Ana gazed deeply into her. Then the dark eyes began to twinkle, like a robin's. The broad shoulders began to shake. Suddenly she sprang up and thrust her hands under the girl's armpits. With a rich, ringing laugh she tossed the startled princess into the air as if she had been a little girl.

Ana set her down on her feet, swung her round by the shoulders and pushed her towards the door into the sunshine.

'What do you see?'

'Your children playing.'

'As you and your brother once played in this same yard. And when these children are grown?'

'You will have others.'

'Will the Dolphin not dance for them as he danced for you?'

Finnglas hung her head. 'Yes. Of course he will.'

'The Dolphin's dance is not a circle but a spiral, drawing us ever closer to the centre of the world. Do we dance it alone?'

'Never. I must join hands with you and with your other children.'

'And when Finnglas reaches the centre, is the ring-dance ended?'

'It is not. There are others coming after me, still dancing in.'

'Dance on to the centre, then, Finnglas of the Horses. And trust what follows to the Dolphin. Look, your foster-father, Nodd, is coming.'

A coracle touched the river-bank, a black speck against the bright water. A man stepped out, and slung a laden net over his shoulder. He came up the meadow with a light but limping step, as though from an old, healed wound.

He stopped before Finnglas and Ana, whistling with pleasure, a little, wrinkled, sun-browned man in a knitted smock. He raised white eye-brows over dancing blue eyes.

'So, daughter Finnglas, you have come home to us again?'

Dark eyes met blue over her head. Ana told him simply of Finnglas's trials. Nodd set down his net of fish before the women. Fish-scales were thickly matted on his bare, tanned feet. He laid his hands on Finnglas's head, and she felt an old peace flow through them.

'I bring you a better gift than food, Finnglas of the Horses. From the Isles of the West. Sleep.'

He led her across the yard to a pile of straw. She lay down, and let him cover her with an oxhide. His fingers rested on her eyes and closed them. The sun fell warm on her face. She slept.

In the farmhouse, Nodd took hold of Ana's hands across the table.

'Well?' he asked.

'I do not know. We will do all that we can.'

24

A small boy's voice woke Finnglas from sleep.

'Mother! Mother! Come quickly! My calf is sick!'

Unwillingly, Finnglas opened her eyes. Dreams of her own childhood, of Melisant, her pony, of her brother's laughter, fled beyond recall. She woke to the grim reality of the present.

She pushed back the oxhide and looked out. The sun was hidden, and grey cloud had crept over the sky. She could see the glow of firelight through the farmhouse windows. The spring day had not far to run.

'Mother! Mother!' The little boy was tugging Ana across the yard. 'The spotted calf is lying down, and his eyes are closed, and he's breathing so noisily. I'm sure he's ill! You can make him better, can't you?'

Ana put her arm round his shoulders. 'I have herbs to cure what can be cured. Quiet now. Don't frighten the little one.'

They disappeared into the byre, and Finnglas was left alone. She looked up at the dark woods above the farm and shivered. Soon night would fall. Somewhere on the far side of the forest, Dubhthac and the nobles and druids would be preparing the sixth trial for her. It seemed as unreal now as the dreams she had already half-forgotten. But the fear was beginning to grow.

She should not have supposed that she could hide from it. Ana had given her food to strengthen her. Nodd had given her sleep to rest her. But no one could take the fear away. It was hers to bear alone. She was Finnglas, the princess, the Tanist. Only she could prove herself the queen.

She did not know where the sixth trial would be. She did not know her way back through the forest. She had lost her companions, her sword, her horse.

Still sleep-slow, searching for what comfort was left, she pushed open the door of the byre. Ana swung round, and smiled deep and long into her eyes, as though she understood everything. She moved aside for Finnglas to see.

The red and white spotted calf lay on its side, struggling for breath. Slime dribbled from its open jaws. Ana knelt beside it and wiped its nostrils and mouth with a wisp of hay. Her hands felt its throat and chest, searchingly, knowingly.

'It shall be well. We have herbs to cure this.'

She stood up, and her hands reached above her head. From the beam hung bunches of leaves, grey-green, brown and withered black. Her fingers moved slowly through them.

'Angel-hair, thankweed, pearlwort, mercyroot, . . . and this. This I call sweetsoul. Let us see how your speckled one likes it.'

She loosened a feathery sprig and handed it to the boy. Their two heads bent over it. The child's small fingers crumbled a leaf. At once a bitter, stinging smell rose from it.

'Ugh! It's horrible!' exclaimed the boy in disgust. 'Why do you call it sweetsoul?'

Ana's rich laugh rolled round the roof. 'When those that are sick call me to be their wise-woman, they do not come to me for my beauty, but for my power. Things are named truly for their actions, not for their seeming. Look at Finnglas. She came to us torn, tired and dirty. Would you think to look at her that she was a queen?'

'I am not queen yet,' said Finnglas in a low voice.

The brown eyes looked deep into hers.

'And this calf is not cured yet. But we have the power. . . . Well, lad, are you going to stand there all night? I have given you what you asked for. The calf is yours. You'll need hot water for a posset.'

The boy trotted across the yard beside her swinging strides, busy and happy now, trusting her completely. Finnglas was left alone. She squatted beside the calf, stroking its gasping throat and heaving chest.

'Don't die,' she begged. 'Hold on a little longer. By tomorrow, all will be well.'

And she knew she was speaking to herself.

The child came back with Ana, proudly staggering under the weight of a small pail. He set it down by the calf's head and lifted the lid. At once an acrid, choking steam filled the byre. Finnglas gasped, as it burned her nostrils and stung her eyes. She sneezed violently and gulped for air, only to feel the bitter fumes strike through her lungs like lightning. Her brain reeled.

Then suddenly she found her eyes were wide open, cleared of all trace of sleep. Her lungs were breathing deeply. Every nerve in her fingertips was tingling with energy. She felt as vigorously alive as if she had rolled in fresh snow. The others were laughing at her face.

'So!' chuckled Ana. 'You have breathed sweetsoul too!'

The calf gave a feeble sneeze, and opened its eyes, bleating with relief.

'Look, Mother!' cried the boy. 'He's better already, just from the smell of it.'

He scooped up some gruel in his fingers, and the calf licked it gratefully. They watched it guzzle until the pail was empty. Then its eyes opened enormously. Its head fell back upon the straw. It gasped once more, then the eyelids fell shut and it lay utterly still.

'Is it dead?' wailed the boy.

'No,' Ana smiled at him. 'He will sleep deeply for many hours. And when he wakes, he will be whole and free from all pain. Stay with him now.'

She stood up and rested her arm across Finnglas's shoulders. 'And you? Will you sleep too?'

Finnglas raised her eyes to her foster-mother's. 'No. I am not a child now, though I will carry your love always in my heart. It was for this you raised me. I must go back across the Great Forest, mustn't I? But I have no horse and no guide and I have lost my way.'

Ana's bright eyes held hers. 'You have never been alone, even in the greatest darkness.'

She looked up at the forest, where the shadows were already thickening. She let out a long, ringing cry, like that with which she called the cows home. Finnglas listened, but she heard only the echoes pealing from the hillside.

'Come. You must eat first,' said Ana. 'Then we will set you on your way.'

They gave her water to wash, and clean, homespun clothes. She sat at table with Nodd and Ana and all their children, and ate baked fish and bread and honey. The children chattered with their mother, but Nodd sat silently beside Finnglas, breaking food and passing it to her. Outside the dusk was gathering, but heavy cloud hid the pattern of the stars.

Finnglas stood at the door facing east.

'I do not know the way,' she murmured.

From the hillside came a single deep bark.

Nodd smiled. 'Where the forest grows thickest, there will be a path. When the night is darkest, there is still light. But only those who have trusted themselves to the dark can tread that path and see that light.'

Ana folded the girl in strong arms against her chest, and kissed her warmly.

'Dance on, and still be dancing at the end.'

'I will,' Finnglas said. 'And promise me there will always be dancing and laughter in this house.'

And she walked away from the firelight and the food and the love.

Nodd walked with her up the dusk-grey meadow, to where the forest sent down its shadows to meet them. He stopped under the first branches. One wrinkled hand held hers. The other rested on her head.

'In the fiercest strife, be most at peace. In your hour of weakness, know secret strength. In deepest loneliness, find your true friends. In the end, there is nothing to be afraid of.'

'I know,' Finnglas smiled wryly. 'It's not the end. It's just the getting there.'

And she kissed him strongly, and walked into the woods.

25

It was fully dark under the trees. After a few steps, Finnglas looked behind her. She could see nothing, not even the glimmer of firelight from the farmhouse.

'Was I really there?' she murmured. 'Did I dream it?'

But the love was still warm about her, the clasp of Ana's arms, the firm grasp of Nodd.

She went on, up the first broad path, where she had ridden so many years ago with her brother, on her first pony, Melisant. In the darkness, the dreams came clustering thickly round her. So there seemed nothing strange in the beat of hooves along the path. Then a dead branch cracked sharply. A horse whinnied in front of her.

Finnglas started violently.

'Melisant!' she cried joyfully. 'Can it be you?'

But the figure standing over her was taller far. A great warm horse's nose reached down and brushed against her cheek. A deep voice spoke.

'No. I am not the pony you once loved and lost. I am Sailte Cloud-Clearer. But when you chose me, you said that in the heat of the day I would bear you nobly, when you were weary I would carry you tenderly, if you fell I would cover you. Will you trust yourself to me now?'

Finnglas flung her arms round his neck and hugged him.

'Oh, Sailte! Forgive me! I did not recognize you. But how in the world did you know where to find me?'

Sailte chuckled. 'It seems you have more friends than you know of. I was guided here. But I came gladly. Mount me now, and I will carry you to the sixth trial . . . if you want me to.'

He felt her body go suddenly still. Her hands gripped his mane.

'You do not have to tell me. Tonight it must be Gormgall the Fair.'

'In the Cave of the White Sow, when the moon goes down behind the hill.'

She shuddered, and buried her eyes against his neck.

'Have Erc and Niall returned with Drusticc?' she whispered.

'No, they have not.'

'Then there is no one to help me now.'

The chestnut stallion had no words to offer. He pressed himself against her, trying to feed her his warmth and strength. At last he felt her grip loosen on his mane. For a few moments she stood alone in silence. Then her voice came small and firm out of the darkness.

'The moon is climbing. It is time to go. Lend me all your speed, Sailte.'

She sprang on to his back. He did not need her heels against his side. He broke eagerly into a trot, then a canter.

'Do you know the way?' called Finnglas.

In the same instant a deep, commanding bark thrilled through the forest. Finnglas swung round. She glimpsed two red eyes burning through the gloom. The great white wolfhound leaped out across their path.

Finnglas grabbed at Sailte's mane and tried to haul him aside. The hound turned in a flowing movement and sprang away up the track to their left. With a joyful neigh, Sailte reached out his neck and galloped after it.

'Where are you going?' gasped Finnglas. 'Do you not fear the White Hound?'

Sailte's laughter echoed through the trees.

'I both fear and trust it!'

And Finnglas remembered how the Hound had driven her towards the sunrise and the House of Ana. She gave herself up to Sailte's wild gallop, and let him carry her where he would. They were flying up a ride now, with Finnglas crouched low over the streaming mane. Ahead of them sprang the wolfhound, its long, lean body at full stretch beneath the branches, like a running moonbeam through the darkest night.

Branch after branch, mile after mile went by. Finnglas lay along Sailte's neck, drugged with his unflagging speed, wishing this journey could go on for ever. She could not see the moon climbing above the clouds. There was only the thud of Sailte's hooves and his panting breath, and the warm strength of his body beneath her. She could not hear the druids gathering on the other side of the hill.

But it could not last for ever. Too soon the night was turning towards morning and the ground was beginning to fall away in front of them. They were coming to the far side of the forest.

The wolfhound stopped, where the first gleam of the setting moon stole in under the trees. It raised its muzzle to the sky and bayed deeply. From beyond the wood came startled cries of fear. The hound turned, and grinned at the horse and rider. Its red eyes sparkled. For a brief moment its tongue licked Finnglas's foot. Then, with a single bound into the bushes, it was gone.

Sailte steadied his weary legs to a trot, and struggled to bring his heaving chest under control. Finnglas sat up. She pushed back her hair and straightened her tunic. The last of the branches gave way to level moonlight. They came out from the soft-floored forest on to open grass.

'Niall?' murmured Finnglas. 'Pangur? Erc? Where are you now?'

But there was only the chestnut stallion bearing her forward. Slowly the charger carried his princess over the grey grass to where two towering slabs of rock guarded the entrance to a valley. The shadow of that gateway fell black upon them us the path dropped suddenly downwards. In that same moment the setting moon went down behind the hill.

In the dark hollow was a darker cave. Under its lowering roof a fire was smouldering. It made the twisting shadows deeper than ever. Outside the cave the faces of the waiting nobles and druids were caught in contorting colours, like ranks of demons. As they drew nearer, the air was heavy with strange, foul scents. Columns of smoke, sulphurous yellow and green, writhed around a steaming cauldron.

In the mouth of the cave, a litter of pale piglets was snuffing. Finnglas picked her way carefully through them.

From the far side of the fire a voice startled the echoes. Once it had been sweet as honey, long, long ago. But age had cracked it, and jealousy had made it bitter.

'So, Finnglas Redhand, you have dared to come to the Valley of the White Sow, after all?'

'I have not returned in my own strength. I do not seek the sceptre for myself, but for my people, and the Dolphin's honour.'

'Then, daughter of kings, let me give you this cup of welcome.'

A whisper ran through the watchers outside the cave. Then a deep stillness fell. Even the piglets were silent.

Finnglas walked alone into the cave. She held out her hand across the cauldron, a small, slight figure in the flickering gloom.

'For this I came. Give me your cup, Gormgall, who was once called Fair.'

A clawed hand stretched out, offering her a leather beaker. Under the stars, Rohan shifted uneasily, so that his jewels jingled. Laidcenn's fingers stroked his harp, as if he told a charm. Only Dubhthac stood like granite, watching Finnglas.

The girl's fingers closed round the beaker bravely. Then she gave a loud cry.

'What trick would you play on me? This cup is empty!'

The echoes cackled with a mocking laughter. The piglets ran squealing out of the cave in confusion, scattering the nobles and the bards. When the noise had hushed, Gormgall had crept closer to Finnglas around the fire. The swaying flames threw a shifting glow on the bent and hooded form but left one side in darkness. A finger pointed.

'I watched you as a child, Finnglas Redhand, that was more a boy than your monkish brother. You played with swords, and learned the right-hand way of courage. But who was there to teach you the left-hand way of wisdom? Could Tomméné, or Manach, or all these sky-struck druids? It is not to be found in the mathematics of the stars, but in the depths of earth. No, daughter of Kernac. If you were our true queen, you would know the dark as well as the light. Nine of the earth's deep charms I have made ready. Eight for hate, and one for love. You shall pour the cup you choose with your own hands.'

She drew a steaming ladle from the cauldron and offered it to Finnglas, chuckling as the girl drew back.

'Did you think it was poisoned? See, it is only boiling water. But *here*, these are the secrets I could teach you.'

With difficulty she stooped still lower and pushed the embers aside. Hidden in the ashes at Finnglas's feet lay a dull and blackened metal bowl. A crumbled powder lay at the bottom of it like a darker stain. Gormgall poured the water hissing over it. The pungent steam wrinkled Finnglas's nostrils. The old woman shuffled past her and woke the brew in another bowl with boiling water. Nine times she moved around the circle of the fire. Each time she filled another bowl. The fumes crept and coiled around the cavern walls. Some were bitter, some fetid, some cloying sweet. And as she bent, and dipped her ladle, and poured again, a cracked chant quavered through the hissing steam.

> 'Hemlock, henbane, hellebore,
> Viper's venom, toadstool's spore,
> Arsenic and antimony,
> Baby's corpse, my servants be.
> She who knows their power shall choose them;
> Be she queen, well may she use them.'

She shuffled back through the smoke and turned up her red-rimmed eyes very close to Finnglas. Knotted fingers gripped the girl's wrist as she whispered.

'Speak true, is not this what you have longed for, Finnglas of the Horses? Choose eight of these, and I am offering you the sleep of peace for ever. The cup that ends all strife and pain. But if you win, all these are yours to use. For all your enemies, a swift and certain death. Drink deep now, daughter of kings. One way or the other, death is in your hands.'

Her eyes gleamed suddenly up at the watchers outside. There was a movement of panic. Even Dubhthac took a step back. When the voices hushed, they saw two heads bent close together in the firelight, the young woman's and the old. Outside the cave, Sorcha raised her staff to the drifting stars and made a strange patterning.

'I have sworn to bring life.' Finnglas broke away and walked to the edge of the fire. She lifted a steaming bowl to her face.

The smell was foul. She put it down quickly in disgust. The next she lingered over. This was sharp, but not unpleasant. The third was sweeter still. But she dared not drink it. Yet one she must. There were six bowls left. From one of these she must fill her beaker, raise it to her lips and drain it down. Slowly she moved around the fire. The columns of twisting smoke hid her from view.

The waiting lengthened. Even Gormgall was silent now, her head thrust forward to the flames, listening intently.

Then, from behind the fire, came a violent sneeze. Next moment a burst of laughter rang through the cavern. Finnglas came striding out into the open, the fifth bowl in her hand.

She drew a deep, gasping breath of cold night air. Suddenly the stars were brilliant over her again. The wind was keen against her face. Once more her laughter pealed around the hollow.

'At the hearth of my fostering I found healing and hope. But I did not know then how rich a gift they were giving me. Yes, from your hand, Gormgall the Fair, I choose this herb of goodness which Ana calls sweetsoul. But all your poisons I will cast on the fire. From this valley of death, I will take only life.'

Without waiting to try the rest, she kicked the contents of eight bowls over the reeking fire. Then, from the one she held, she filled her beaker to the brim. She raised it triumphantly. Her eyes were fixed on Gormgall's face as she tossed it to her lips.

The burning liquid seared her throat. All her senses were on fire. She saw the hate blaze up in Gormgall's eyes. She smelt the stench of poisons in the flames. She heard the cauldron crack and the steam shoot foully past the stars. The pigs screamed in the sudden darkness. Then the fierce heat struck through her veins like lightning to the heart. Night came rushing over her as she fell.

26

Niall and Erc stopped in their tracks before the white cat. The sun turned cold.

'Are we too late?' Niall cried. 'Has Finnglas fallen to the druids?'

'Tell us quickly,' Drusticc commanded. 'What ill has been done here?'

Pangur poured out his tale.

'. . . And when we heard where she was, Sailte set out across the Great Forest to find her. Since then I haven't seen a hair of either of them. I don't even know if she entered Gormgall's cave . . . or if she came out alive. Oh, what has become of them?'

Niall bent down and picked up an alder rod from the floor. 'What is this you have here?'

'The seventh challenge. It came just now.'

He read it out in a shaking voice. 'If Finnglas dares, let her come once more to meet the druids at the Stones of Choosing in the darkness before the dawn of Beltaine.'

There was an odd sparkle in the abbess's eyes. 'Praise be! It seems, in spite of you two, we still have hope. The princess may yet be alive. If she had fallen at the sixth trial, would Dubhthac not have claimed the victory by now?'

Niall looked desperately round. 'Where *is* she? Why doesn't she come?'

'Hm! For three long nights she must have been asking the same question about you two,' said Drusticc crisply. 'Let us trust that she has friends we know nothing of. We must prepare ourselves for the best and for the worst. If she still lives, tonight Finnglas and Dubhthac must come face to face at last. And each should fear the other when they meet.'

'There was something else,' mewed Pangur suddenly. 'The druids have cried a message through all the land. Tonight is

Beltaine Eve. At sunset, every fire in the kingdom is to be put out. Every hearth must be cold tonight. No flame will burn again until the fire is kindled by the new Ruler at tomorrow's dawn.'

Drusticc raised her eyebrows. Her smile was dancing now.

'No fire, indeed! When the three Dark Days are drawing to their close? Tomorrow is the High Feast of Arthmael's Rising, when all his followers will be gathering to celebrate.'

'Celebrate?' wailed Pangur. 'How can we celebrate now?'

'Have courage still, little Pangur!' Drusticc tossed him into the air. 'With the help of true friends, has Finnglas not won six times? And these runaway slaves, you say, are in the woods with Ranvaig?'

She swung round to Niall and Erc and gave her orders swiftly. 'Niall, Pangur will guide you to their camp in the forest. We shall want all the firewood the slaves can carry. Be on the beach with them when darkness falls. And tell the slaves, tomorrow on Arthmael's Feast, when Finnglas is queen, they shall be truly free.

'Erc! We shall need a boat. The largest you can find. But do not let yourself be seen borrowing it. Go quickly, all of you, and do not fail Finnglas this time.'

No one argued with Drusticc. A moment later, Niall and Pangur were running across the meadow. They disappeared into the hazel thickets. Erc strolled along the shore, glancing with seeming carelessness at each of the craft he passed.

Drusticc stood alone, looking at the tumbling waves. Rising and falling. In and out. But there was no leaping back, no threshing tail, no laughing eye. She did not need these signs.

'Be with us through the night. Give us courage to the last. And joy in the morning.'

She turned and went into the house. The gaming-pieces were scattered on the floor. The abbess picked up two of them from under the table and set them on the board, facing each other. The red druid and the white hind. Then she sat down to wait.

Her head nodded. She did not hear the soft, slow-pacing hoofbeats on the grass. She did not hear the low whisper of Sailte, 'Finnglas. Wake up! Gormgall is defeated. You are safe home again.' She did not hear the grateful murmur as Finnglas slipped from his back and came sleepily towards the door.

A shadow fell across the threshold.

'*Drusticc!*' And then Finnglas was running across the room.

'Eh, what's that?' Drusticc struggled awake. 'This body of mine is weaker than I thought. Too much fasting and not enough praying, by the feel of it.'

'Oh, Drusticc! Praise be to Arthmael, they've brought you to help me!'

'You've been a pack of fools. I was never necessary. All the help you needed was already round you. Did you think that Arthmael would not have seen to that?'

'I know that now. I should have trusted him. I have found friends better than I dreamed of.'

'Well, since I am here, I might as well stay and see the end.'

The light died in Finnglas's face.

'The seventh trial! Drusticc, can you help me now?'

'No. At the Stones of Choosing, in the darkness before dawn, you must meet Dubhthac face to face.'

'I . . . alone?'

'Were you ever alone?'

'But you are telling me . . . that this last trial is *mine?*'

The abbess rested her hands on the girl's shoulders.

'I do not know what he will challenge you to do. But this I warn you. You are in mortal danger. Tonight you will stand in peril of your life, and your soul.'

Their eyes met steadily.

'Then I must get ready,' said Finnglas, 'while the light still shines.'

27

The slopes of Rath Daran were busy with excitement. It was the Eve of Beltaine and the Choosing of the Ruler. Horses were being curried, armour polished, clothes washed and dried in the April sunshine. Horns and drums burst out from time to time, as though they could not wait for morning. Even the sheep and cattle were noisy, scenting summer and sweet mountain grass.

While Finnglas dressed, Drusticc stood in the doorway, watching the scene. Her face stilled. She turned her head swiftly. From the further hill, by the Stones of Choosing, a solemn chant was rising. Already the distant figures of druids were moving round it.

The sun went down behind Relig Rí, reddening the water round the Island of the Kings. Drusticc laid a hand on Finnglas's shoulder.

'There is much to be done. But I shall be back before midnight. Hold fast to your faith and your courage.'

Finnglas walked across the stones to the sea's edge and stared out over the greying water.

'Niall? Erc? Pangur Bán?' she whispered.

What was that? Was something moving, out there in the twilight on the lough? There was no break now in the long, rolling waves. Had she imagined it? She watched dusk settling on the water, hiding the island where they had laid her father.

This had been the last day in which the Dolphin was hidden from them. The night was coming in which he would break the power of life and death. The dawn would find him leaping from the sea into the sun, in the Great Dance. But would she live to see that dawn?

At midnight the drums began to beat. The moon had already turned towards its setting. It glimmered on Drusticc's white robe as she hurried across the meadow. It glimmered on something else small and white, running in front of her. Pangur Bán leaped across the threshold and into Finnglas's lap.

She laughed and hugged him against her face.

'So you are true to the end, Pangur Bán! Have you come to wish me luck or to say goodbye?'

'Oh, don't, Finnglas! Don't!' he begged.

She stood up and faced Drusticc in the doorway.

'I am ready now.'

She had dressed herself with great care for the last trial. A rich, red dress, embroidered with crystal and silver, that made a whispering music as she walked. Shoes of the softest leather. Her hair was braided with gold and starred with hawthorn blossoms. She looked like a queen, yet not quite an earthly one.

But she placed about her shoulders an old, stained cloak of black pony-skin. It was stiff with salt and tattered from many gales.

'I left this land as a great princess. But I came back in rags, wearing this gift my friends made for me. They were few but very precious. Niall the monk, Erc the fisherman, and little Pangur Bán. They have saved my life more times than I can count. It is for them I would be queen. And I will wear this proudly until they lift it from my shoulders and dress me in the seven-coloured plaid of the High Queen, or till it wraps me in my grave.'

Drusticc looked her up and down.

'They tell me you won a royal sword in your trials.'

'A fine blade, but a better scabbard.'

'Yet you are not wearing it now.'

Finnglas looked at her sharply.

'They call me Finnglas of the Horses now, not Finnglas Redhand.'

'Tonight you must do battle for your father's kingdom.'

Finnglas buckled on the sword belt silently. Then she slung the harp she had won across her shoulder, and hung from her belt the flask of healing she had taken from Gormgall.

116

'So! I am fully armed. Sailte Cloud-Clearer is waiting for me. And my chariot is harnessed for you and Pangur.'

'Then there is only one thing left. Your father's kingdom. Let us go and claim it.'

28

The moonlight was alive with shadows. Horse-trappings jingled, people whispered breathlessly. Somewhere on either side of her would be faces she knew. But there were no cries of greeting. Only the drums beat out their rhythmic summons from the Stones.

Sailte Cloud-Clearer carried her proudly. He never swerved or stumbled as he paced the maze that climbed around the hill. The moon went down behind the Forest, and the waters of the lough turned from silver to black. From the summit the drums beat faster, like a sleeper beginning to wake.

Finnglas alighted. There was a grey, unearthly starlight on the hilltop, close to the sky. She could not tell Dubhthac's face among the ranks of white-robed druids massed round the summit. But she did not need to. He was there, standing alone, beyond the Stones of Choosing, where only the Ruler may stand, and one whose wisdom ranks higher than any chief.

There was a strange black mound beside the Stones. Was the darkness playing tricks with her eyes? Had light flashed from it for a moment, reddening the pendant on Dubhthac's breast and the knife in his hand, on the night when all fires were put out but one?

She wanted to turn back to the lough for help, but she steadied herself. They greeted each other.

'I have come, Dubhthac of the Golden Knife, as you challenged me. Six trials I have passed. Tomméné, Manach of the Hosts, Laidcenn the Harper, Rohan of the Bright Chariots, Sorcha Clear-Sight, and Gormgall who is called the Fair, all have put me to the trial. They have all owned me queen. These Stones will shout and my name will ring through my father's kingdom. There is only your challenge left. I come to take it.'

'I greet you, Finnglas of the Horses. Long is the time you have been away from us. Strange are the new paths you have sailed. Yet you have proved that you remember well the old knowledge. You have shown courage, skill, wisdom. When the sun rises you may yet be our queen.'

Her eyes flew to his face in astonishment. She had not expected this. Surely it was Dubhthac's trial she should most fear? Then, as his eyes smiled down into hers, a horror struck her.

Tomméné, Laidcenn, Manach, Rohan, Sorcha, Gormgall. She was younger than all the others of the royal house. Ignorant of almost everything a queen should know. What if Dubhthac, for that very reason, had chosen her? What if he *wanted* her to be queen?

Panic swooped through her soul, like bats tumbling out of trees. There was darkness in her mind, blacker than the night that enfolded her. Till now, she had thought that the worst thing that could happen would be that the tribe might not cry her queen. She had thought that to fail this trial would mean Arthmael's defeat.

Now something more terrible showed itself to her. What if she passed the last trial? What if Dubhthac let her take the crown, and with it set his evil hold on her? What if she was queen and the Old Powers proved stronger than her love for Arthmael? Could he twist her to work against the Dolphin?

She looked swiftly towards the sea. Drusticc stood behind her, like a tall white spear, with Pangur crouched on her shoulder.

'There remains one trial yet, Finnglas Redhand. Between the Old and the New is a deep divide. Tonight I challenge you to cross it. Have you brought your sword?'

She stiffened, wary now. It was the second time that question had been asked tonight.

'I wear it at my side.'

'So. It is well. And has the blade been blooded?'

'You know it has not. I chose it as much for the scabbard as for the weapon. It is the royal sword of good government. Long may it stay sheathed and the land at peace.'

'We are a warrior tribe. Your father led us to cattle raids and

119

war. The earth is hungry for blood. And the sword, you say, is unbaptized?'

'It is as clean as when it came from the smith's anvil, washed in the water that cooled the smoking steel.'

'That is well. Then the earth may be satisfied, and the old custom fulfilled.'

'You speak strangely. What custom is that?'

'That every kingly blade that leaves the forge must drink its first blood from a living sacrifice. The High Chief's own hand must do this.'

Finnglas felt her own blood drain from her cheeks. A loud murmur raced round the ranks of the nobles. Had they known this? Had her own father done it? Had Luis Sunfire known, as he hammered the blade? The whispering was running through the tribe now, like shivers of fear. Did the old ones remember a time when the sacrifice had been human blood?

Finnglas was glad that in the starlight no one could see the ripple that ran down her red dress in a long shudder. She could not find an answer. Her chilled lips were suddenly stiff and her throat cold and dry.

But Dubhthac's voice was rising, so that the whole tribe should hear, chanting now, taunting out his triumph, because, however the princess chose, the druids must win.

'Draw that sword now, daughter of Kernac. We have brought you a fitting sacrifice. The white, unspotted one. You who would be queen, plunge your clean blade into this pure heart. Then drink from that blood the life of the tribe, and bid us feast with you at the first fire of Beltaine. Then the land and all your people shall name you, *Finnglas of the Horses*.'

She heard, and yet she did not hear him. As the druids stepped back, she saw the heap of firewood stacked for the Beltaine fire. She saw the great cauldron hiding the sacred turf and smelt the smoke. They were leading before her something slender and white. Thin-legged, kicking, struggling against the ropes that bound it. Faint whimpers came from its muzzle that should have been piercing cries of terror. Appalled, her hand froze on her sword hilt. Tomméné had once offered her this horse as her own. She was looking into the face of the pure white colt.

29

The whole tribe was staring at her in the starlight. She heard their indrawn breath. They knew she stood on a great divide, between Dubhthac's ways and Arthmael's.

'Well, princess? For the life of this tribe, will you make the sacrifice?' Dubhthac smiled.

'And if I do not?' But she knew the answer, even before she asked.

'Then you are no true queen of ours. You must surrender that sword. And the land shall drink deep from richer, human blood.'

The crowd moaned around her. But something soft and warm rubbed against Finnglas's ankles. She dared not look down at Pangur, lest the druid should think she was afraid. But courage began to flow through her cold, stiff limbs.

She smiled into the terrified eyes of the colt.

'Do not fear, little brother,' she said soothingly. 'You shall go free with the first stroke of my reign. Or we shall die together, you and I, and our bonds shall be loosed for ever in the Great Dance that knows no end.'

Then she turned to Dubhthac, and her voice rang out before all the people.

'No, Dubhthac of the Golden Knife! Your time is over. The ways of blood are gone for ever. I come to you not with a sword but with a song!'

And laughing, she flung her hand from the pommel of her sword to the minstrel's harp. Her fingers swept the strings and found a pure, true note. As it throbbed to the dark heavens and the pulsing stars, it woke an echo in the Stones of Choosing. The music chimed out across the hillside like a peal of bells, rocking the sky, ringing out over the lough.

As if in answer, a sudden shaft of gold pierced the darkness. Fire blazed on Relig Rí, a great bonfire on the Island of the

Kings. Joy leaped in the dead of night, when every fire was put out, save for one hidden turf smouldering in the druids' cauldron.

Drusticc's voice thundered triumphantly. 'Arthmael is risen!'

Pangur squeaked, 'He has come back to the world!'

A howl of horror rose from the throats of the massed druids as they faced the sea. Dubhthac screamed with a sound that seemed to be dragged from the very Stones.

The flames were throwing jewels over the water. Dark figures were leaping and dancing in front of the fire. Snatches of singing echoed across the lough.

'Stop them!' shrieked Dubhthac. 'Stop that fire!'

'It's Niall!' yelled Pangur, dancing on white paws in excitement. 'It's Niall and Erc and Ranvaig and all the slaves. They've lit Arthmael's birth-fire! This is the day of his rising from the dark depths. The day of his dancing. His fire will burn till the sun rises. It will burn for ever!'

'Never!' roared Dubhthac. He whirled round on the druids. 'Never! That flame must be killed, smothered, flattened, extinguished into the very blackness of the earth. Run, you dolts! Race! Gallop! Fly! If the Dolphin's fire still burns when the new sun rises, when the first rays touch the Stones, then the victory will be his. The cat speaks true. The Dolphin will conquer, and the old ways go down into the darkness for ever.'

Even while he spoke, the sky was paling, and the first light, that was not quite silver, was washing the stars from the night like a flooding tide.

The great crowd of yelling druids rushed past the Stones, burst through the bards, scattered the common people. Running, stumbling, leaping down rocks, seizing horses, chariots, tumbling down the hillside. They hauled boats from the shore, grabbed oars, struggling to get across the slowly-filling, silvery stretch of water that was just beginning to glow with the first hint of dawn.

And on Relig Rí, the island of the graves, the great fire of life danced higher and higher as the leaping figures piled it with branches. A sudden flame flared for a moment on the huge form of Niall as he heaved wood up from the beach. And

Dubhthac fastened his eyes on the monk as the druid fleet rowed furiously across the water.

All the time, the stars were fading in the sky, and the edges of the clouds were touched with rose. The cold wind of dawn blew between the Stones. But Finnglas did not feel it. Her whole being now was in her eyes, staring out over the lough, over the island, to the far horizon, where the whole ocean was being gilded by a greater fire.

A great shout of joy rang from her lips.

'Look!' she cried, pointing.

30

Arthmael was coming, as she had known he would. Out of the deep, up from a darkness they would never know. From battles that can not be spoken of, from pains that it would sear the soul to hear. From love that bore the whole weight of the world's dying and carried it, with his scars, back to the day.

He rose into a dawn that was not yet sunrise. He leaped from the ocean, black, shining, new and strong. He threw a triple somersault for joy and crashed back into a welter of laughing spray, and the whole sky broke out its banners of scarlet and gold for him. He dived through the still-grey waves before the spreading dawn.

Then the sea came alive around him. Emerald mermaids with golden combs. Sapphire and purple mermen surfaced. Dolphins and porpoises, humpbacked whales and grinning sharks. The whole shimmering, shining, storming shoal raced for the shore, with Arthmael leaping at their head.

As the wall of foam burst into the sea-lough, the druids were rowing frantically for the island. Then Arthmael was in among them, his great tail twisting and lashing in a loving rage. The curraghs and skiffs went weaving, spinning, capsizing in their desperate efforts to escape. The druids screamed and cursed. They were floundering in wet wool robes in water and weeds. The ring of whales and merfolk, silently smiling, closed in around them.

Dawn was touching the edges of the shadowed land. The flying tumult of water was turning from black and white and taking all the colours of the rainbow.

'The fire!' shrieked Dubhthac, tumbling over a shark. 'Their power is growing. We must put out that fire!'

With a terrified glance at the sky that would soon be blue, the druids fought for the shore, kicking the mermaids aside, dodging the whales, clambering up the stones. All Kernac's runaway slaves came rushing down to the beach, brandishing branches. The druids raised their staves, and the two forces closed and clashed in a grimly bitter struggle.

The white-robed druids were chanting as they fought. Their long ranks were gaining. The ragged slaves were being forced back. Ranvaig was at their head, wrestling bare-handed, but Dubhthac threw her aside. The fire was leaping in his eyes as he ran through the graves. He did not seem to feel the pain of blows. He was struggling desperately to reach those flames on the summit, and put them out for ever.

Suddenly, above Kernac's tomb, a huge figure barred his way. Niall held a mighty log in both his hands.

'Stop! Not one step further!'

Dubhthac bared his teeth and rushed forward.

Niall heaved the log above his head. One moment more and it would split the druid's skull.

Arthmael lifted his great scarred head from the water, and all the seafolk held their breath.

Dubhthac gasped. But still he came on. Niall's eyes went sideways to his hands, that had once painted the glorious pages of the Gospels. From the Hill of Choosing, Drusticc, Finnglas and all the tribe gazed down silently.

The log wavered. As Niall hesitated, Dubhthac's staff dealt him a cracking blow to the side of the head. The young monk went reeling to the ground. And Arthmael smiled.

With a yell of triumph, Dubhthac rushed on to the fire.

As the morning neared, the flames had almost died out. All the wood had burned away to a soft white ash. Only one slight figure was left in front of it. Erc gripped the last branch in his hand and faced Dubhthac. He knew he was holding Finnglas's life and Arthmael's victory in his grasp. Once more he saw the druid's staff rise to the sky. Behind him the last flame whispered and went out.

Erc swung his branch towards Dubhthac. Then, with a laugh, he tossed it away from him on to the fire. As the fresh flames leaped up to meet the morning, Erc threw himself full-length at Dubhthac's feet.

The startled druid tumbled off balance. His eyes blazed with horror as his staff went spinning through the sky and dropped down to add fuel to the new flames. He grabbed for a hold, found nothing. Before all their eyes he went rolling, somersaulting, shouting wildly down the hill. Over the grass. Past Niall, who was staggering to his feet. Across the beach, too fast to stop. A rising wave caught him as he bounced and dropped him in the cold salt sea in front of Arthmael.

As the water closed over Dubhthac's head, the Dolphin lifted his laughing face to the sky and whistled.

And summer came. The whole surface of the lough took fire with scarlet and rose and dancing gold. On the hillsides all the flowers opened their eyes, yellow and white in fields of vivid green. The horses shook out their manes and broke into a canter, with Sailte at their head. The birds gave a great shout of joy. And the new sun rose, as though for the first morning in creation.

Light touched the Stones. The fighting ceased. Suddenly there was silence, save for the birdsong, and the crackling of the flames round the druid's staff. Then a great groan burst from Dubhthac's followers, a cry of grief and loss. They rent their robes and hid their faces in their cowls.

The High Druid rose from the water, spluttering. Seaweed was tangled round his ears. His face was white. But the sunlight was laughing in Arthmael's eyes.

'The battle is over, Dubhthac. Come and swim with us now.'

'Never!' swore the druid, and cursed him.

Playfully, Arthmael knocked him over and picked a crab out of his hair. His laughter had faded into a coaxing smile.

'Come on, Dubhthac. You've lost. Won't you play with us now?'

'Never!' choked Dubhthac, struggling to his feet.

Arthmael dived between his knees and sat on him. A tear glistened in the corner of the dolphin's eye.

'Dubhthac. Can't you laugh with us? Try!'

'Never! Never! Never!'

The High Druid toppled head first into a coracle. He seized the oars threateningly. 'Get away from me!'

This time Arthmael did not move to stop him. Sadly he watched the druid row away, till he had dwindled to a tiny, lonely figure on the lough. The rose and scarlet of dawn faded from the water. The waves threw back the brilliant blue of morning.

Then Arthmael stood up on his tail and shouted in triumph. The watchers on the Hill of Choosing heard his voice ringing across the water from Relig Rí.

'Well, go on! What are you all waiting for?'

And the Stones of Choosing echoed with his voice.

The whole tribe seemed to wake, as if from the bonds of a spell. Pangur sprang on to Drusticc's shoulder and called aloud, 'We have won! We have won!' And suddenly everyone was turning to each other, and they were all laughing in the new May morning.

Tomméné strode forward, black-whiskered, magnificent in his warrior's gear. His torques of gold and his weapons and armour flashed in the sunlight as he cried to them all,

'Well, people of the Summer Land. You have seen seven battles won. How do you say now? Who will you have to rule you in Kernac's stead?'

And all the tribe shouted to the listening heavens,

'FINNGLAS! FINNGLAS OF THE HORSES SHALL BE OUR QUEEN!'

And the Stones of Choosing rang true with one name and sent the echoes back to Relig Rí.

But Finnglas called in a firm clear voice that carried across the lough,

'I claim this realm. But before you all, I declare that the victory and this kingdom belong to Arthmael. Finnglas of the Horses shall rule you now in his name. And with my first act I do what he would do.'

With one slash of her sword, she cut the white colt free. Then she cried to the slaves on the Island of the Kings,

'Kernac's servants! Choose your own life now. You may stay with me, or take passage back to your homes. You are slaves no more.'

'Hm!' Drusticc snorted to Pangur. 'I told you she didn't need me.'

Old Conn was waiting beyond the Threshold, with the sceptre and the golden crown in his hands. But Finnglas turned away from them. Before the whole tribe she bowed low to Arthmael. And out on the lough, the great Dolphin stood up on his tail and saluted her. She bowed once more to all her people. Then she came through the Stones of Choosing to take her crown.